Upton Sinclair

OUR LADY

OUR LADY

Upton Sinclair

Reprinted by Frederick Ellis
8000 E. Girard, Suite 507
Denver CO 80231

ISBN 978-0-9793363-0-0

OUR LADY

Contents

Admirers of Upton Sinclair, of whom I am most certainly one, will be delighted to see *Our Lady,* the novel which Mr Sinclair considers his best, returned herewith to print.

I believe in the intrinsic greatness of this book, and I can well understand the author when he says: "There is a saying that every author has one book which he especially loves, and *Our Lady* is mine." The book has haunted me, just as it has him — its strange beauty, its awesome conception, and its form of fantasy! Never before has Mr Sinclair handled his material with such tenderness, and with irony so compassionate rather than wrathful. We can see now in these pages the prophecy and promise of those mellow masterpieces, the "Lanny" books, which have belatedly won the Pulitzer Prize. For it was the series, rather than *The*

Dragon's Teeth alone, that really received the accolade.

It is a parable for moderns that *Our Lady* is to be seen as one of the best literary works of our era. "I asked to see the future of myself and my son," Marya complains, "and nothing I saw has anything to do with us." In these words is the point of the parable, and the indictment of our whole contemporary civilization — that there is nothing in it all which the mother of Jesus could recognize as having to do with her son, whose sayings she kept so carefully in her heart.

I may be pardoned for repeating in this place, as my conviction today, what I wrote of *Our Lady* in a review in the New York *Herald-Tribune,* when the book made its initial appearance:

"There is irony here, sharp and bitter. The conversations between Marya and the Notre Dame Professor, disclosing Marya's utter innocence of all things so central to Christian dogma, are devasting in their penetration into the question of what has happened to Jesus and His gospel.

"But tenderness and compassion are none the less the prevailing temper of the book. There seems to be a new Sinclair in these pages — one greater and kindlier than we have known before, yet still as uncompromising in conviction."

Lastly, may I make bold to thank the present publishers for this new edition. They are rendering a service to booklovers the world around in restoring this masterpiece to print. *Our Lady* deserves a great public. I am sure it will be a long-lived one," has said that distinguished critic, Mr Lewis Browne. This time, I am sure, the book is going to receive the attention it deserves.

JOHN HAYNES HOLMES

June 15, 1943

Chapter One 15

MY FATHER'S BUSINESS

I

MARYA stood in the doorway of her home, watching her oldest son walk down the stony path which led through the little valley. He went without looking behind him, as one who had put his hand to the plow and might not turn back. His shoulders were slightly bowed, as if with the burden of his thoughts. She knew so well his way of walking, with his eyes fixed on nothing. She followed him with her yearning; her soul cried, "Come back! Come back!"— but she knew that he would not hear.

It was a morning in early springtime, and the floor of the vale was covered with soft and tender green. This verdure was to her as the flesh of her first-born. The flowers, bright blue and pink and golden, were the little love-thoughts which had started in his soul, and which hers had plucked and cherished. The glory of the fruit-tree blossoms were the robes in which her fancy had dressed him. The songs of the bluebirds were his first murmurings, the music from the larks in the sky were angels singing welcome to the newborn babe. These stirrings of sense and soul are the secret treasure of young motherhood, and whatever may be her later cares and sorrows, she keeps the memories buried somewhere in her inmost heart.

Now this first-born was grown to manhood, and was going his way into the world. Her eyes followed him, to the point where he would pass out of sight. She knew that part of the journey, but the rest was unknown to her and full of perils vaguely guessed. While her hungry eyes devoured his every movement, her frightened soul fed itself upon despair. When he passed the threshing floor of Simon ben Zoma, their nearest neighbor, her inner voice was crying: "It is forever!" When he passed the wine press which the vineyardist Jaddua had hewn out of the rock, she was whispering: "I shall never see him again!"

Lovely was that land of Galilee in springtime. Flowing waters, bright abundant verdure, soft contours — nature had done her best. The little vale opened out into a shelf, and there lay the village of Nazareth, each of its streets a terrace made by men's labor, beautiful with fig and olive trees, date palms and vineyards. Fifteen blue hills half-circled the plateau. To the north lay tall Mount Hermon, still tipped with snow; to the west purple Mount Carmel, with the great sea beyond it; to the east wooded Mount Tabor, rounded so that the poets of Palestine compared it to a bosom. Why could not a man be happy in such a place? With a home, and a treasure of love in it, why must he go wandering into a madhouse of cruelty?

He had a duty which she did not understand; he heard some inner voice, unknown to her. He had spoken sternly, even harshly, to his mother. The sound of his sandals on the path had died away, and his figure grew smaller to her eyes. He came to the place where an orchard cut him from her sight, and he passed it without turning to wave to her, doubtless without even thinking of her.

II

MARYA turned into her house. It was a one-room cabin, made of grayish-brown clay. It had one door, no windows, and a flat roof. Its furniture consisted of a table and two benches, two blue-painted chests for clothing and other objects, and a box on which were set several pieces of pottery. This unusual amount of furniture was due to the fact that her husband, Josef, had been a carpenter, and her first-born, Jeshu, had learned the trade, and still now and then followed it.

Various utensils and tools stood against the wall of this humble home: a water jar, a wine jar,a broom made of twigs bound to a stick, a spade having an iron-tipped point, a reaping hook. There was no graven image or ornament of any sort, and no attempt at decoration; the beds were straw, and Marya's was covered by a sheep pelt, a part of her dowry, aged, but still treasured. In one corner was a wooden peg to which she tethered a she-goat at night, and in another corner a peg for the sheep; both of these creatures now had their young, and their presence meant that the floor was alive with fleas. If the Lord had made any place without fleas, it was surely not in Palestine.

There was no way of heating such a home; on winter nights in this hill country you wrapped yourself in a robe. By way of lighting there was a small flat dish filled with oil, and having a groove in which a wick was laid. The cooking was done outside; the stone fireplace was in a yard or court, perhaps twelve feet square, in front of the cabin.

Outside the house, Nature expounded her lesson that beauty and utility can be combined. At one side an ancient fig tree spread its branches thirty feet in every direction; each twig was now a branched candlestick pointing to the sky, having at each tip a bright flame of green. From one side of the house stretched a grape arbor, its leaves half-grown, its sprays of tiny blossoms filling the air with sweetness such as no king could purchase for his concubines. At the other side the carpenter's shed was built against the house, and in the rear stood olive trees, ancient, with gnarled trunks, and branches which never lost their multitude of little silver leaves.

Such was the home in which Marya had labored for thirty years. In that time, lying on the sheep pelt, she had borne nine children and raised six of them. She was now a widow in her late forties, which was old age in that day; her hands were knotted with toil, her sinews stood out like cords, her face was lean and deeply graven. But she had been fair when first she had come to this home, and now to the discerning eye her features revealed kindness, wisdom, and love.

She did not know how to read or write. She had never had a day in school; but from her husband and her sons she had learned texts, some of them being words of precious import. She had observed nature and human life, and applied ancient sayings to modern experiences. Moreover, it had befallen that her first-born had developed great powers of mind, and she had watched these unfolding; she had questioned him, and kept his strange sayings in her heart. He had gone much to the "house of learning," the room in the synagogue where the holy books were stored; so in his talk had been the ecstacy of the psalms, the majestic anger of the prophet Isaiah, the strange visions of the Book of Daniel. He would leave his work and wander over the hills, pondering these lofty matters; the mother, tending the beasts and preparing the food, traveled with him in her thoughts, and would question him when he returned.

So she was not just a peasant woman; nor was her village the mere collection of mud hovels it appeared to the traveler. When Marya went to the well, as she did twice a day, carrying her cruse on her head, she had opportunity to hear talk, not merely about Nazareth, but about strange events in many parts of the world. This land of Galilee had been fought over by armies, and among its crowded dwellers were Syrians from the north, Egytians from the south, Babylonians and Chaldeans from the east, Greeks and Romans from all the seas.

Less than an hour's walk distant lay the town which the Romans called Sepphoris, lately restored and having a royal palace and a garrison. Through this town passed the Via Maris, "the road of the sea," which led from Accho on the coast to the valley of the Jordan, and thence to Damascus, the great city of Syria. By this stone-paved route went Roman soldiers, and caravans of camels and asses, and heavy carts drawn by oxen, hauling the marble pillars and carved pediments for the new city of Tiberias, which the ruler, Herod Antipas, was building for the glory of the emperor who kept him on the throne.

Yes, the people of Jerusalem might sneer at those of Galilee, calling them "'amme-ha'aretz," that is to say, "people of the soil;" they might mock their way of speech, lacking the much vaunted "lishna qalila," the light and tripping accent of the smart set of the city, who had nothing to do but dress themselves in fine raiment and chatter to one another. But the "people of the soil" had the Law and the Prophets, and if they did not cultivate worldly arts, it was because the faith of their fathers was good enough for them. They lived sober and godly lives, cultivating their fields, observing the Gentiles without paying them the compliment of imitation.

III

MARYA had two children yet unmarried: Jeshu, her eldest, who had just set out on a journey, and Joses, her youngest, a stripling, bright-faced and eager. Even now Marya's brother, the head of the family, was occupied in negotiations having to do with Joses' betrothal; but the lad had not been told of this, and was occupied at the carpenter's bench behind the house. Jeshu had taught him the trade, and left him his precious tools; a crude saw, a chisel, a wooden mallet, a knife, an adze, and a measuring stick two cubits long, marked off into fractions thereof.

Joses was not depressed by his brother's departure, because it meant that Jeshu would have adventures in the great world, and some day would come back and tell about them; also because he had left a partly-finished chest, and the lad had in mind certain details of his own conception. When it was completed, an agreed price would be received, and the money be buried in a corner of the hut, and used to buy corn at harvest time.

At midday the mother placed upon the table some cakes made of wheat and oil, and baked the previous day upon a hot stone; a lump of goat's cheese; some fresh onions out of the garden; and two small bowls of milk. That was their meal, and at this season of the year their steady diet. While Joses ate with abundant appetite, he sought to beguile his mother out of her mood of sorrow; she on her part sought to instruct the last of her sons, that he might not be lured into the strange and dangerous paths of his eldest brother.

To this peasant woman of ancient Galilee the outside world was a place of such wickedness as could hardly be put into words. The promised land of the Jews was become a part of the Roman empire, and its rulers were men whose adulteries and poisonings and murders by sword or dagger made familiar gossip. Before Joses was born these rulers had taken a census of all the Jewish people, something which had occasioned uprisings and slaughters; now the tax gatherers came, more surely than the locusts, and demanded a share of every product of the land, and if it was not paid, the people were driven from their homes or thrown into prison. Herod Antipater had his father's vices with none of his competence; under him the Jews were mocked and their sacred things defiled.

Why did the Lord permit such events? It was a question which every Jew asked himself, and debated in long conversations. Some purpose the Holy One must have in mind, but it was not apparent to His children. He had promised to set free Israel, and it was certain that He would keep this promise; but why did He wait so long?

Joses asked these questions, and his mother answered as best she could; but he was no better satisfied with her replies than his brother had been years ago. "Yes, mother. You say it is Satan who makes these evil men and gives them power. But surely Jahveh has more power than Satan; and why does He permit Satan to have his way in the world?"

Marya was divided in her mind between pleasure at the lad's keenness, and fear lest he become a rebel like Jeshu. Earnestly she explained the peasant philosophy, the caution gained through many generations of suffering. The great ones, whether they were in heaven or on earth, were beyond control and even beyond understanding of the poor. "They do not permit us to ask them questions; and it is safer not to ask even in our own minds." In the Aramaic tongue, as used by the Jews of Galilee, the word "adon," lord, applied not merely to God, but to any person, Jew or Gentile, who bore the appearance of wealth or power. So it was easy for Marya to impress the lesson of submission to authority. Said she: "All I ask of the great ones of the earth is that they do not know that I exist."

"But mother," argued Joses, "we are not ground-squirrels, that can disappear into a hole."

Said the mother: "The ground-squirrel in the talons of the hawk is not more helpless than the poor man in the hands of an official."

IV

THIS was not called going to school, and yet it was a kind of education; it was history as taught long years before there were books. Marya had grown up in the days of Herod, called the Great; she told how this great one had caused the murder of his brother-in-law, his uncle, one of his ten wives, and three of his sons. When Marya was a girl in her father's home, King Herod had died, and many of the Jews believed that the time of the prophesies had come, and they began to preach the advent of the Messiah; for which the new king, Herod Antipater, had taken two thousand of them and nailed them upon crosses.

"They drive iron spikes through your hands onto a tree," said she. "They hang you up in the sun and leave you till you are dead, and the only kindness they can do is to drive a spear through your heart. To me it seems natural to wish that this should not happen to one of my sons."

"But mother," argued the lad, "the Lord has told us that we shall some day be free."

Said Marya: "The Lord is hard upon mothers. We wish to keep our sons; and I do not know how this great desire can have got into our hearts unless He has put it there." By way of precaution she added: "I say no more than that" — a plain indication that there was much more in her heart. "Yehe-shmei-rabbo-m'vorach!" she exclaimed quickly; meaning: "Let His great Name be blessed."

Joses pondered all these sayings. "Mother," he remarked, "you are unhappy because Jeshu speaks so many rebellious words. Do you not realize how many you yourself have taught him?"

"Ai, ai!" exclaimed Marya. "It has always been the privilege of the poor to grumble — at least in their own homes. But what does he do, my first-born? He goes out into the market-place, and tells the people that the rich are buzzards. How can such things go on?"

"Are the rich afraid of the words of a carpenter in a village of Galilee?"

"An arrow can pierce the vitals of a rich man as quickly as those of a poor man, and the rich know it. The crowds are beginning to flock to Jeshu, and the rumor of his preaching is going through the land. Now he goes to meet this madman, Johanen, and what good can come of that."

"Is it really true that Johanen is mad?"

"Ai, ai! How can I know? I hear what people say — that he is a Nazarite, and does not cut his hair, and he wears the pelt of a camel, and lives in a cave, along with the jackals, and his food is locusts and wild honey. Now he comes to the banks of the Jordan with a practice of dipping people into water, a senseless thing."

"Is it true that he is a prophet of God?"

"Our unhappy land is full of those that say they are prophets of God; and how shall a poor woman know which to believe? All that we can do is to obey the Law, and keep the feast days, and ask that the quarrelsome and noisy ones shall let us alone."

Joses pondered, while munching a young spring onion. "Tell me mother, is it really true that Jeshu communes with the Lord?"

Marya's mood changed suddenly. "Your brother is one of the most truthful of men; and that which he tells me I can only receive with respect."

"But might he not be mistaken, mother?"

"Anyone that lives will sometimes be mistaken. I can only say that my first-born is a wise and good man."

"He does not tell you what the Lord has revealed to him?"

"He tells me only that the time for telling is not yet."

V

IT WOULD perhaps have been the part of discretion for Joses to drop this subject. But when your own brother, that has lived in the house with you all your life, takes up the practice of going out under the olive trees and standing with upraised hands, praying to God most of the night — and when he tells you that God has spoken to him — can you help feeling curiosity about it? When your brother keeps the secret, can you help feeling slighted, and left out of the family affairs?

"Doesn't he tell you anything at all, mother?"

"Only what you yourself have heard him say, that he must be about his Father's business; also that the end of the world is coming soon."

"I wish I knew what to think about that. If it is true, why should I go on trying so hard to learn to be a carpenter?"

"We must live until the time the Lord pleases."

"What do you think about it, really?"

"The evil deeds that I have seen or heard tell of in my lifetime have surely been enough for me; if I should hear that they have exhausted the patience of the Lord, I should not be surprised."

"What would He do with us, mother?"

"If He ends the world, I suppose He will end us. Of what use would we be to Him?"

"Of course," mused the lad, "if we didn't exist, we wouldn't know about it, so it wouldn't matter."

"The Pharisees have a strange idea," said Marya; "that when they die, God takes them into heaven with Him, and they live there forever."

"But what do they do there?"

"I have never heard that. They are generally learned and important people, as you know, so doubtless they will praise God loudly, and wear robes with broad fringes, as they do now."

"Does it mean that only the Pharisees will be taken to heaven?"

"I do not know, my son. Men teach strange notions these days. I heard that a Zealot had stabbed a man to death for preaching wrong doctrines. Many cruel things happen — that is why I cannot endure to see my first-born go out into the world."

Marya's grief came over her in a fresh wave. She had barely tasted her food, and now she pushed it away.

"Here he has a home!" she exclaimed. "Here his father and his grandfather lived before him. He has a trade, he can always earn a good living. For fifteen years I have been begging him to choose one of our lovely maidens; but he will not look at them."

"Perhaps the Lord has told him," suggested the lad.

"The Lord has sent me no balm for the aching of my heart. I think of Jeshu among strangers — going into desert places where there are robbers —"

"There are robbers everywhere, mother. People say they divide with the officials."

"Hush, my son!" Marya glanced fearfully toward the door of the cabin.

Her eyes came back to the stripling, her baby, now growing up so fast. He had beautiful black eyes, large and expressive; his face was lovely, his skin like a girl's. But soon he would be a man, and would insist upon going his own way. He might become bold, like Jeshu, and speak his thoughts in the market-place, for all to hear. He, too, might begin hearing the voice of the Lord!

Said the lad: "If the end of the world is coming, as Jeshu says, I cannot see that it matters greatly who is robbed or who gets the money." Then with a smile upon the girlish face, he added: "It will be a surprise for the Romans — just when they have built so many new marble cities! Will God destroy these cities, or will He give them to the Pharisees?"

Chapter Two 37

THE DARK-MEATED ONE

I

MARYA washed the bowls from which they had drunk, and swept the floor of the cabin, and saw to the beasts which were tethered out to grass. Such woman's work might cease when the Lord brought the world to an end, but assuredly it would not cease before that. The same being true of the need of men and beasts for water, Marya put the pitcher upon the top of her head, having arranged her hair for a pad, and walked down the path to the village well.

Here there was always company, women sitting and resting and discussing the affairs of the world. There were some who had seen Jeshu arrive in the village, and go out with five companions by the road to the Jordan valley. Through a gap in the hills to the east one could see this far place, and again Marya followed her son with her thoughts.

Travelers had come back from the Jordan; so all the village knew that Johanen was "dipping" great numbers of people in the river; also that he was preaching, in the somber, threatening fashion of the Hebrew prophets. "Now also the ax is laid unto the root of the trees; every tree therefore which bringeth not forth fruit shall be hewn down, and cast into the fire." There was a report that Roman soldiers had set out from Sepphoris with orders to take him; one could not be sure if this was true, but Marya was ready to believe the worst. Her heart, like her water pitcher, was heavier on the return journey.

Close to home, her need of relief grew extreme; she must unburden her soul to some one of her own age and experience. She stopped at the cabin of the ben Zoma family, knowing that at this hour Sara, the mother, would be seated at her task of weaving. She found also by good fortune Sara's cousin, Rachel bath Rachmiel, come upon some errand. These three were all of them grandmothers, and made a goodly company, lamenting the state of the world, the breakdown of authority, the wild ways of the younger generation, their failure to honor and obey their fathers and mothers that their days might be long in the land which the Lord their God had given them.

It chanced that Rachel's brother, young Simon Peter, was among the number who had gone with Jeshu to hear the preaching of the new prophet. Rachel too was distressed, and a little disposed to blame Marya's son, as being the elder, and leader of the company. "He is a rebel," said Rachel; and Marya answered that it was the sufferings of the people which drove him to rebellion. She wept as she defended her first-born against the sin of arrogance; Rachel wept in her turn as she admitted that Jeshu was a good man, in spite of his lack of respect for the scribes and the priests, and his strange refusal to keep the feast days. They agreed that they were living in a terrible time; they shuddered as Sara told what she had heard about the many crucifixions in Judea, now a separate province from Galilee, ruled by another son of the wicked old Herod. As usual, the sons were worse than the father.

These were Jewish women, and it was their practice to express their grief. Marya wrung her hands as she told her fears for her first-born, whom she described in the phrase of her ancestors as the "petach valda," the "opener of the womb." The tears ran down her cheeks and she exclaimed: "I cannot bear it! I cannot bear it!" But these, of course, were mere words. Having used them, women whether Jews or Gentiles went on and bore what they had to bear.

II

GROPING for a way of escape from the pain of uncertainty, Rachel bath Rachmiel, wife of a very respectable candlestick maker of Cana, remarked presently: "I have thought that I would consult a soothsayer, if perhaps I can learn something of what will happen to my brother."

"Oh!" exclaimed Marya. "That is forbidden by the Law!"

"But does Jeshu always keep the Law?"

Fresh tears came into the mother's eyes. "He does not keep the letter, but he keeps the spirit."

"But he rebels! And I too wish to rebel sometimes!"

It was a thrilling vista of conversation which opened out before them. Many, both men and women, were breaking the Law against having traffic with soothsayers and magicians. It had been known in Nazareth that the wife even of a learned scribe, honored by God, and his praises proclaimed by the angels, had stolen away to a fortune-teller by night. Sara's sister, Miriam, had once been told that her family would have great good fortune, and a few days later her husband, digging a well, had come upon a jar containing strange coins such as no man in the town had ever seen. Alas, the fortune-teller had omitted to mention that the Roman officials would take the treasure away from the finder!

It was not that any Hebrew questioned the existence of demons and other infernal powers, and of spells by which these could be compelled to serve the will of men. Whenever the Jews had conquered another tribe, the gods of that tribe had become demons; everyone knew they existed, and that they were powerful; but Jahveh, the one God of the Jews, was All Powerful, and His chosen people were commanded to trust in Him, and to spurn all the false gods and have nothing to do with their rites.

But Jahveh was remote, and perhaps now and then forgetful, while the demons were all around you, especially at night, and it was an ever-present temptation to put some of them to work for a worthy cause.

Sara and Rachel knew the names and habits of many of these demons, and also they knew spells and magic actions which would control them. Thus, if you passed between two women whom you suspected of witchcraft, you brought their powers to naught by whispering to yourself: "Agrath, Azelath, Asiya, Belusiya are already killed by arrows." If some demon got into your beasts and interfered with the proper delivery of their young, you would have to say: "Burst, cursed, dashed, banned, be Bar-Tit, Bar-Tema, Bar-Tena, Chashmagoz, Merigoz, and Isteahan."

Now Rachel bath Rachmiel advised Marya how to lift the burden of anxiety from her soul; she could find out what was going to happen to her first-born, and might even find out if there was any truth in his strange notion that the Lord was going to bring the world to an end before those who heard his words had passed from the scene. Rachel had a friend whose friend had tried a spell, and told of many wonders accomplished. All that Marya had to do was to take some first-born creature — the Jewish ritual always laid great stress upon the "petach valda," the "opener of the womb." Marya must kill the creature, and cut off its head, and prepare it with salt and spices, and she must place under its tongue a gold plate which had graven upon it certain magic formulas; then straightaway the tongue would speak and answer all questions as to the future.

Unfortunately there were several objections to this program. In the first place, Marya's son Jeshu was sternly opposed to soothsayers, declaring that our Heavenly Father did not subject His children to the whims of Gentile demons. In the next place, Marya did not own a gold plate, nor did she have the money to buy one. Finally, Sara had only a vague report of the content of the magic formula, and of course it is known that no formula works unless you get it exactly right.

They continued to pursue this perilous subject; lowering their voices and gazing about uneasily, because the hour of twilight was approaching, when demons are abroad. Presently Rachel was telling about a sorceress who lived some distance from Nazareth, at a lonely spot on the road to Cana. No one knew just how she lived, but of her powers there could be no doubt, for she had told a certain woman that her child would die soon after birth, and it had happened exactly so, and even that the body had developed dark spots. This woman was what was known as a Nabataean; she came from the land which had been the home of the Queen of Sheba, and which now is called Arabia; its people were known to the Hebrews as the "dark-meated ones."

This woman from the deserts had brought with her certain of her own black devils, and Rachel told fearsome stories about these. The most powerful of them was Zar, and his mother was known as Umm-az-Zar, and she was in some ways even more dreaded than her son. If you went to this sorceress, you must take, not merely a first-born, but also a sprig of mint, which had some ritual significance to these people who dwelt in tents made of skins.

Rachel strongly advised Marya to take this means of ridding herself of her anxieties; but Marya shuddered, and said she would not dare to do it, that Jeshu would never forgive her. She went away from the old wife's conference whispering an orthodox and proper Aramaic formula: "Yitgadal-vi'-yitkadash-shmei-rabbo!"

— that is, "Magnified and sanctified be His great Name."

However, Rachel, who had lived long and grown wise in the ways of Jewish women, called after her: "It is the first house that you see in the rocky glen to the right just after you pass the pomegranate trees before the home of Isaac the woolcomber."

III

JOSES had wheat porridge for his supper, and ate it cold, because his mother had been gossiping with the neighbors when she should have built a fire. But he was a good lad, and it sufficed him that she had been getting news about Jeshu and his companions. They talked about their loved one and where he would be now; he could hardly have reached the Jordan, thirty miles or so away; he would be staying in some humble hut like this. He taught the people and they heard him gladly. He took with him neither scrip nor purse; people gave him what was needful, and he said that the laborer was worthy of his hire.

After they had supped, they stood up and said their prayers. They prayed as Jeshu had taught them, simply, in their own words. Their prayer was that Jeshu might be safe; that no robbers might trouble him and no Roman soldiers take him, but that he might live to do the will of his Father which is in Heaven, Amen.

Joses went to bed; a process which was simple in those days. He had never heard of a toothbrush, nor of the idea of different clothing for night. He had only to take off his sandals, and cover up his feet from the fleas. His pillow was a lump of rags; he slept soundly, having worked all day in the open air, and taking no thought for the morrow.

The mother sat upon the threshold of her cabin, flooded with light from a silvery half-moon. That moon was shining also in the valley of the Jordan, and perhaps Jeshu stood beneath it, his arms upraised, praying. He would be asking, not for his own safety, but for his fellow men and the lessening of their woes. Marya thought: "What if the Lord be hearing him, and paying no heed to me?"

Jeshu declared: "Thy Heavenly-Father knoweth." He prayed: "Thy will be done." But that was not enough for Marya. She wanted her own will to be done in respect to Jeshu's safety; so now she wrestled with a fearful temptation. If the Lord was too busy to attend to this matter, surely He could not reasonably object if she made it her concern. Surely the great Master of the Universe, Ribono-shel-olam — Marya said the syllables all run together, like the clerk of a court swearing a witness — surely this all powerful One would pardon the extremities to which a woman be driven by maternal love.

She got up and went into the hut. The goat was tethered in one corner, and the sheep in another, each with its young snuggled against its belly. The kid would not do, because it was a female; the baby ram was the ordained victim, and Marya stood gazing down at it. She trembled, not merely with superstitious fear, but with honest peasant emotions of a practical nature. It was a hard price to pay, one-half their increase for a year. But she knew that no smaller offering would suffice; the sorcerer, too, was worthy of his hire.

She went out again and sat in the moonlight and debated it. She might pay the price and get nothing. That was something which happened often to the poor in trading; it was one reason their lives were so filled with anxiety, and they spent hours and sometimes days debating a single bargain.

Suppose she did learn Jeshu's future, what could she do? Her fears told her that it would be no good news; she would have her mourning in advance — and would that help her? Could she hope to avert the fate? She was a woman of firmness, and in many cases had been able to guide her family. She now saw herself going to Jeshu, and by the sheer pressure of her grief breaking down his resistance, persuading him to come home and stay.

At least she would try. Nothing else meant much to her. If evil befell him, and if she had failed to avert it for the price of a newborn ram, she would never forgive herself. As for what the Lord might do to punish her — she feared the Lord, but she loved her son, and her love was stronger than her fear. Amen.

IV

MARYA went into the garden and broke off a sprig of mint, and tucked it into her girdle. She returned to the cabin and threw a shawl over her head, and took up the little ram from its mother and tucked it under the shawl; she knew it would be still, and no night-prowler would guess that she carried such a treasure.

She awakened Joses, something not so easy. "Come," she said, "we must go on a journey." When he was slow about getting his eyes open, she added: "Jahveh has spoken to me." It was an untruth and a fearful one, but Marya might as well be hung for a flock of rams as for one.

Joses was on his feet, filled with curiosity. "How, mother? And when?"

She replied: "We must go, and quickly. No one must know. It has to do with Jeshu."

As soon as he had fastened his sandals she started down the stony path, and he followed. They went through the valley, and along one of the terraced streets of the village. All was dark, save for the moon; all was silent save for barking dogs, and the shrill yelping of jackals in the hills. The latter had their young now and were hunting fiercely; woe to any small beasts that strayed!

Demons would be hunting also. Marya could not be sure how Jewish demons would react to her choice of a dark-meated one, so she walked quickly, and for the demons of Galilee she said: "Abinu-shebashomayim," which is very old Hebrew for "Our Father in Heaven;" also "Kabeil-t' filoti," which is Aramaic for "Accept my prayer." It is hard to know how to pray to a God who is all-powerful and all-knowing — and at the same time may not be minded to do what you desire!

They passed out of the village by the valley road which led toward Cana. It became a pass between hills, dark and fearsome. Shadows stood out black and sharp, and every jagged tree-stump was a possible enemy. Marya hugged her baby ram tightly, and murmured her prayers faster, and Joses followed close upon her heels.

Cana was her birth-place, so she knew this road well; she knew the sheds of Isaac the wool-comber, with the pomegranate trees in front, loaded now with scarlet blossoms. A dog rushed out at them, but Joses had a staff and kept him at a distance, and they hurried on. There was a ford, with a tiny stream that would be dry later. This was "the rocky glen to the right;" they turned into it, and there was a hut, and Marya whispered: "I cannot take you with me. Sit here, and keep watch."

"What is it, mother?" pleaded the lad, afraid; but she said no more. She went to the cabin and knocked, and when a voice answered, she pushed open the door and entered.

V

THE dark-meated woman sat upon a cushion in the center of her cabin. She had a sort of iron basket, and in it a little charcoal fire. This in itself was impressive to Marya, for in the circle of her friends was no one who could afford such luxury. Nabataea was a hot land, and this woman was not used to winds blowing from snow-covered mountains. She was clad in a saffron robe with black stars and crescents on it. The unflickering red light brought out her sharp features, and made her seem awesome. She was old, but her hair was thick and black, and she herself almost black.

She kept her seat; doubtless being used to people stealing into her cabin at night, and having studied how to impress them. "What is your wish?" she asked, with a foreign accent not easy to understand.

"I want a spell," said Marya.

"What kind of a spell?"

"I want to know the future of my first-born."

"Why does he not come himself?"

"He — he is not here," said Marya, hesitating. "He is on a journey."

"I cannot tell the future of a person who does not come to me," said the Nabataean. Then, in the line of her business she noted that her visitor had something beneath her shawl. "What have you brought?"

"A first-born ram," answered Marya.

"Let me see it."

She took the tiny creature and examined it, then set it upon the ground, where it stood upon its feeble legs, bewildered. It baa-ed once for its mother, then stood trembling.

"I have brought also a sprig of mint," said Marya.

The woman pointed to a cushion on the other side of the brazier. After the visitor had seated herself, she demanded: "What do you wish to know about your son?"

"First, if the world is coming to an end, as he believes."

"Who is this son?"

"I would rather not tell," stumbled Marya. "He does not approve."

"You are afraid of my spells?"

"I am a poor woman, and afraid of many things."

The soothsayer pondered. "If the world comes to an end, it comes to an end for you as well as for your son. It is the same thing."

"I suppose so." Marya was confused by anxiety, and hardly able to think.

"What else do you wish to know?"

"I wish to know what is going to happen to my first-born, whether it be good or ill."

"If ill happen to him, you will be sad, is it not so?"

"That is so."

"If good comes to him, you will be happy. So, if my spells reveal your own future, you will know his."

That seemed a reasonable statement, and they discussed their bargain. The witch-woman was precise and business-like; she could not afford to have a dissatisfied customer, who might get her into trouble with the authorities. They must decide the question of exactly what kind of spell. Did the visitor know any of her familiar spirits?

"I have heard of Umm-az-Zar," said Marya, timidly.

"Umm-az-Zar comes not for women."

"Does Zar come for women?"

"He might come for you. I feel his presence. He whispers to me about your son. This man has a strange future, and so have you. You will be surprised by what Zar will reveal. Shall I proceed?"

The mother was too frightened for speech. She sat twisting her hands together, awaiting the onset of the fearful powers of darkness.

"You understand," persisted the stranger, "I guarantee nothing. I shall be in the hands of the powerful ones. I become entranced, and I do not know what they do or say. You, also, will be in their hands. Speak politely to them, I warn you."

"Oh, surely," stammered the woman of Nazareth. "I wish them no evil! I will be grateful for their help. Tell me this: shall I know afterwards what I have seen?"

"You will know what they let you know. I will ask them to take you into the future. You may behold wonders which people of this time have never seen, and will not believe when you tell them. But I do not guarantee. Is it understood?"

"I agree," said Marya.

VI

IT transpired that Marya herself must take part in the calling of this demon. She had to learn certain Nabataean words, and say them at the proper moment. The enchantress made her recite them, until she knew them thoroughly. Then the Nabataean reached into a bowl by her side and took out some powder and threw it upon the charcoal. Puffs of dark reddish smoke arose, and a strange pungent odor stole into Marya's nostrils. The sorceress waved her hands, and uttered harsh, gutteral words, and the smoke began to writhe and coil.

Against the wall of the cabin stood an image, something which the commandments of Moses forbade Marya to have in her home. It was an image of a god rudely cut in black stone, and its top was flat and smeared with oil and dried blood. Marya had failed to notice it before; now it was wavering in the smoke, and she thought it was Zar himself coming to take her into the future.

Beside the woman lay a drum, made by stretching the dried bladder of a beast upon a frame of thin wood. It was small, but enough for a secret rite. The woman struck it glancing blows with a little stick having leather on the end. She began chanting barbarous words, swaying and nodding to the beating of the drum, and every pulse of it set Marya's heart to pounding with new fear. She, a Hebrew woman, was disobeying the Law of her fathers, putting herself into the power of a dark-meated demon from the desert. She dared not even pray to the Lord while she felt the dreadful powers taking possession of her soul.

Above the smoke now loomed a vague but monstrous form; and suddenly the witch-woman ordered: "Speak!"

So Marya, in a trembling voice, whispered the words she had learned: "Art thou Zar?"

Said the stern bass voice: "I am Zar."

"Male or female?"

"Male."

Said Marya: "I obey. What dost thou desire of me?"

"Blood of the sacrifice," replied Zar.

Quickly — for demons are well known to be impatient — the witch-woman took a sharp little knife and slit the throat of the ram over a basin. She dipped her fingers into the hot gushing blood, and threw it into the flame, where it steamed and hissed, and the odor of it rose with the smoke. That was Zar's part of the feast; the carcass would be roasted by the woman on the morrow and eaten by her — a most convenient part of the ceremonial. But there was nothing suspicious about this to Marya, for the priests of the temple had the same practice with the first-born of the flocks and the first fruits of the vineyards and the fields.

"Art thou content?" demanded the witch-woman of her demon.

"Sleep!" ordered the stern voice, and at once her head fell forward upon her bosom and she was still.

"Woman of Nazareth!" proclaimed the voice. "Arise and come!"

Marya felt herself taken by the arm and raised to her feet. Her knees trembled so that they would hardly hold her. The strange odors and dreadful sights made her dizzy. Suddenly there came what sounded like a clap of thunder in her ear; she swooned and sank into a heap upon the cabin floor.

Chapter Three

THE GLADIATORS

I

WHEN Marya opened her eyes, she was in bright sunshine, sitting on a grassy sward and leaning against what seemed to be a stone pillar. At first her mind was in confusion; but as it cleared, she realized that this was a place unknown to her. It appeared to be a city, and there was a great crowd of people, all strangely dressed. At once she thought: "It is the future!" This had the effect of calming her mind. She had been told that she would behold wonders, and the promise was being kept.

The first wonder was this concourse of people, all walking rapidly, and nearly all in the same direction. It produced an odd effect, as if a river had turned into human beings. Or was it that human beings had been bewitched and turned into a river? Marya speculated upon these ideas.

She noted that there were a great many chariots, and these were moving in the same direction — a river of chariots. Stranger yet, they were moving of themselves; there was not a single horse or ass or ox or camel to be seen. The chariots resembled boxes, or little houses, smooth and shiny, of beautiful bright colors; they rolled silently, a solid river of chariots — it must indeed be powerful magic. The road was wide, smooth and clean as no road ever dreamed by Marya; the vehicles flowed in the center, and the people made two slower rivers at each side.

Marya noted the peculiar costumes worn by these people of the future. It was hard to tell the men from the women, because none wore beards; to her this meant that they were all Gentiles, and she wondered what had become of the Jews. Never for a moment did she forget Jeshu, and herself as Jeshu's mother. How could she find out anything about good Hebrews in this strange Gentile place?

The men wore their robes divided into two at the legs; or one might say that each leg wore a separate garment, and each garment was like a straight knife-edge in back and front — the oddest effect, as if it were not human beings walking, but figures cut out of wood. Each man had an odd-shaped box on his head, and all the people had pale, smooth, expressionless faces, and moved like automata. More and more it seemed to Marya that this could not be a real world, but some jest which the malicious dark-meated one was playing upon a daughter of Israel.

Still worse were the women! Their robes were short, revealing their legs in a most shocking way. Their arms were bare in many cases, and their faces painted, so that their lips were crimson wounds. Marya could draw only one conclusion as to women of such an aspect. The thing which puzzled her was that there were so many of them. She saw no children, and wondered if the people of the future came into their world full grown, by magic. Obviously, if there did not need to be any mothers, all the women could be what only the worst of women were in Galilee.

There was a vague hum in the air, and Marya got the impression that it came from the river of shiny chariots in which the boxed-up people sat. Then came a louder sound concerning which she could form no idea, except that it might have been produced by a locust the size of a mountain. She looked up into the sky and saw a thing — she did not know whether it was a chariot of fire which the Lord was sending to take her out of this evil world, or whether it was some enormous insect which preyed upon the boxed-up men and their harlots. But neither men nor harlots paid attention to it; and after it had circled several times and done no harm, Marya decided to take it for granted like everything else.

II

NEITHER the Nabataean nor her familiar spirit had given Marya any instructions as to how she was to behave in this world of the future; and apparently nobody here had received instructions as to her reception. For a while she watched the river of hurrying people, and made certain that no one was paying any attention to herself. She ventured to get up on her feet; and finding that this did no harm, she made bold to join the river.

One or two of the people glanced at her with curiosity, but it was a brief glance, and had no menace in it. Apparently they were intent upon their own affairs; or could it be that they were really not living creatures like herself? Anyhow, it seemed to be safe to walk among them, and the visitor from Nazareth walked. There were shops along the side of the street, filled with a variety of goods, but it was seldom that anyone stopped to buy, or even to look. Marya decided that this throng must be bound for some common goal, and be occupied in their minds with that.

Ahead of her appeared an enormous structure, with a high, smooth stone wall and a level top. The stream of people was flowing to this place; and when she got there she saw a fence of wire, and gates through the fence, and tunnels through the wall, into which the streams disappeared. She made the guess that it was some sort of amphitheatre. She knew about such things, because the Romans had built a stadium in Sepphoris, and she had heard that there was a still bigger one in Caesarea. She could even figure out that the people at little booths were buying tokens of admission; she knew that those who went to the Roman games bought little clay disks, having numbers upon them indicating their seats.

To a woman of Nazareth, "games" meant cruel gladiatorial combats in which slaves and barbarians killed one another. It was a thing which every good Jewish woman held in utter abhorrence; indeed, Jeshu had refused to work upon the stadium as a carpenter, holding it such a place of evil. Marya, passing one after another of the gates, marvelled at the size of the structure, at the numbers of the men of the future, and at the fact that they all took their harlots to the public games.

She came to a place at which there were double gates, and a wider tunnel through which chariots were driven into the arena. There was a crowd here, but Marya no longer had any fear of it; she realized that everyone was occupied with what was going on inside. Apparently it was in this world of the future as in the great cities ruled by Rome; strangers were free to walk about and see the sights.

The vehicles going into the stadium were large and of curious designs; they had platforms upon them, and on these platforms were things to be gazed at: trees, arbors, little houses, enormous animals; one was a horse made of brightly painted wood. All were gay with bright colored cloth, with flags and streamers, and flowers larger and more showy than Marya had ever seen.

The people riding on the platforms were not dressed like the crowds she had followed on the street. They wore vari-colored costumes, some even resembling those of Marya's own time; thus she saw Greek and Roman ladies, more than one with a golden crown upon her head. She could not tell whether these were real queens who were being honored in the games, or whether it was a kind of festival in which people wore costumes of various lands and times.

The visitor from Nazareth was used to celebrations. The Jews had their Feast of the Tabernacles, in which the family lived in leafy booths, and made themselves beautiful in the sight of the Lord, and gave Him thanks for the harvest. Perhaps, thought Marya, this was no cruel Roman holiday, but something polite and friendly, according to the practices of a happier time. She was interested, but more and more puzzled as to why she should be here. She had not come to see any sight, but to find out about herself and Jeshu; and what could all this have to do with them?

III

NEAR Marya stood a man wearing a dark blue costume, with a silver shield upon his breast; she judged that he must be a high official. Gradually she became aware that he was paying attention to her, and this made her uneasy, for she was prepared to learn that these were sacred rites, not open to a peasant woman.

Suddenly the official spoke to her. "Are you looking for your float, lady?"

The words, of course, meant nothing to Marya. But the tone means something in all languages, and she realized that the man was friendly. She shook her head, saying: "Lo meyvin," that is, "I do not understand."

"You don't speak English?" said the other; and again she shook her head.

The official studied her. He had never before seen the costume of a woman of ancient

Palestine, a voluminous dress made of undyed wool and tied at the waist with a leather girdle; voluminous sleeves, a hood in back, and a shawl over the head. The man beckoned to an attendant at the gate, and said: "This lady seems to have missed her float; and she don't speak any English."

The attendant tried a few words of some other language on Marya, but it made no difference — she still said: "Lo meyvin." Finally the attendant said: "I suppose she can go in on some other float."

The procession of vehicles had come to a momentary halt. The "float" in front of them was a platform with a wooden hut upon it, and a carpet made to imitate grass; sitting in front of the hut was a man in a bright green coat, and carrying a knotted club in his hand. His face was stained a fiery red, but he was an amiable-looking ruffian, his face wearing a perpetual grin. In his hat was a green feather, and in the buttonhole of his jacket a large flower with three green leaves. Seated around the hut were several fair maids, likewise clad in green.

The attendant escorted Marya, and the crowd made way. "Pat," said he, "this lady has missed her float. Will you take her with you?"

"Sure thing," said Pat. "She kin be me owld mither."

The attendant signed to Marya that he was offering her a ride. Wishing to do whatever was pleasing to these men of the future, she permitted herself to be helped up beside the amiable ruffian, where she looked perfectly all right, except that her dress was not green. However, there were a number of three-leaved flowers made of cardboard fastened upon the hut, and one of the fair maids took two of these off and pinned them to Marya's dress. She did not know the ritual significance of this, and could only hope it was nothing indecent or unworthy. She smiled politely, in accord with the mood of the maid, and of the spectators, and of the festival occasion.

IV

THE procession started up again, and Marya's magic platform rolled slowly through the wide tunnel of stone. When they emerged, Marya found that it was just as she had guessed, an amphitheatre. It was of such size as she had never dreamed; the vast tiers of seats appeared like the fifteen hills around Nazareth; the massed people seemed greater in number than the dwellers in the towns of Galilee.

She had every opportunity to make an inspection of this crowd. There was a road all the way around the arena; the procession followed it at a slow pace, no faster than a walk. Thus all the spectators had a close look at the "floats;" there was laughing and cheering and handclapping and waving of handkerchiefs. Marya understood that she had been made a part of this; it appeared that they were being kind to a visiting stranger, and she must show her appreciation.

She could no longer doubt that these were real people. The men, in spite of being boxed up in clothes, waved their hands and shouted loudly; the crowds shouted all together, in a way which caused volumes of sound to roll back and forth across the arena. Marya saw that there were great numbers of young people, and they were laughing and happy; they wore bright clothing, and looked to be rich. The peasant from Palestine wondered, were there no poor people in this world of the future?

There were bands playing, loud, crashing music, astonishing to a stranger. Marya had heard the music of horns; on New Year's day the priest blew on a ram's horn; but she had never heard anything like these enormous, bellowing things, with openings bigger than a man's body, made of brass polished so that in the sunlight it blinded her eyes.

Marya had lived a limited life, and had no general curiosity. It was not for her at her age to gad about, whether in space or in time, and stare at strange sights. She had come to get some definite facts, and now she kept thinking: what has this to do with me and with Jeshu? She was used to the idea that dreams were symbols, and had to be interpreted. She thought: "I am riding about in a chariot among rich people, being received as one of themselves. Does that signify good fortune for me and mine?"

Some two score vehicles made the entire circuit of the amphitheatre. Overhead roared several of the sky-chariots, and each had a long tail trailing out behind with letters on the tail. A weird-appearing giant insect, with four fans that went round and round, came down close to the field, and Marya would not have been surprised to see it make a swoop and carry off a victim. Another fiery demon let out smoke from his tail, making curves and symbols in smoke. Manifestly, this was enchantment of a most powerful character.

Little balls of bright colors were released from the throng and went floating up into the air. Doubtless they were prayer-balls, carrying messages to the gods of these people. There were others that went up a great way and then burst with little puffs of smoke; were these rejected prayers? Other prayers looked like green and purple and scarlet serpents highup in the air; they wriggled this way and that, and jumped as if they were being shot at with arrows. Marya understood that the shouting, singing, hand-waving, and blowing of trumpets and horns must have to do with the escape of these prayers, or with some struggle going on among the various heavenly powers.

Then came another development, most amazing. Out of the sky a Voice, of such volume that it filled the whole world. Marya's heart leaped — it could be nothing but the Voice of God. If all the people in this place had fallen down and put their foreheads in the dust, she would have understood, and would have joined them. But she could not see that anyone paid any attention to the Voice. Was this a Gentile god? Or had the dread Jahveh of the Hebrews chosen this gay and prosperous people of the future?

V

WHEN the chariots had completed their round, they halted by the entrance tunnel; the persons who had ridden in them alighted, and the chariots were driven away. When the last of them had departed, attendants wheeled into place several high frames of metal pipe and mounted on wheels, which had been standing at the edge of the roadway. These frames had rows of seats upon them, and were placed in front of the tunnel entrance and made fast.

The green-clad man gave Mayra his hand and escorted her to a seat. At her left hand sat a lovely young woman in a white robe, with bright golden hair, a gold crown upon her head, and a gold sceptre in her hand. She looked once at her strange neighbor, then looked away. At Marya's other side sat a row of four gentlemen wearing black costumes made of the finest smooth cloth, their coats having high collars buttoned tightly about their necks, and smooth white collars inside these. Evidently they were persons of dignity, perhaps rulers of this city of the future. They did not look at Marya even once.

In the centre of the arena was a field of grass, marked off into long strips with white stuff, and at each end were two white posts with a crosspiece high up between them. This disturbed Marya by its resesmblance to a gallows; she wondered if the losers of the games would be hanged here — or possibly those who failed to fight to the taste of the crowd. Or were they perhaps to give men a chance to escape from wild beasts which were to be hunted? She could only wait and see.

The gaily painted wooden horse had been hauled out into the arena; also the green-coated man was there with several others like him. Presently the side of the horse opened, and out popped half a dozen soldiers — Marya knew these at once, for they had helmets and cuirasses and short deadly swords like the Romans. She was anxious as the soldiers attacked the men with clubs; but she discovered that it was all in play — instead of shouting for blood, the crowds laughed. The green men ran this way and that, and someone turned loose a big dog which chased the soldiers and tumbled them over.

Then came into the field a little donkey, ridden by a man with a padded white suit with red spots on it; his face was also painted red and white, and Marya wondered what new kind of demon he might be. The little donkey warmed her heart, for donkeys at least were not magic, but familiar home sights. Her family had owned one in more prosperous days, and she remembered his moist, warm muzzle, and his back that the children loved to clamber onto.

This one in the arena was a trained donkey, which did all sorts of tricks; the man rode the donkey and the donkey rode the man, and the donkey bit the man in the place where he sat down. But the Jewish grandmother did not enjoy this fun because her thoughts had fled back to ancient Palestine. Was it day-time there, and was Joses still waiting for her out by the pomegranate trees near the hut of the sorceress? Or had he thought to go home and milk the goat and the sheep?

VI

EVERYTHING was cleared off the field, and the Voice of God began to speak rapidly and with excitement. Suddenly the band struck up, and there came a mighty roar from the throng, and Marya saw that a gate had opened at one side of the arena, and a troop of men came running into the field.

She knew at one glance that these were the real gladiators. They were mighty men, and made still bigger by the armor they wore, all the way from helmets to greaves below their knees. Giant fighters, in very truth; as they ran they pranced like young horses which have been fed upon grain. There were forty or fifty of them, and they spread over the field, and raced about and waved their arms. They had large balls which they hurled at one another with amazing force, and they caught these and galloped about with them in a fashion that seemed quite mad. The sound of the crowd was like the great storms which sometimes roared over the hills of Galilee. Also the Voice of God kept on bellowing. Marya felt herself battered by this tempest of sound.

Most surprising of all was the row of four dignified black-clad gentlemen at her right. She had picked them as rulers of this great city; and here they were on their feet, shouting so that their faces became scarlet. They had produced little green flags and were waving them in the air; there were green flags and streamers all over the stands. Marya realized that the imitation flowers she was wearing must signify that she too was a partisan of the green gladiators.

She noticed that the queen with the golden crown and sceptre remained quiet, and that great numbers of others did the same. The explanation came in due course; for after the green gladiators had romped about for a while, they retired to one side of the arena, and there fell a hush, followed by an even louder storm of sound. Gates had been opened at the opposite side of the arena, and another army of gladiators came charging out, exactly like the first lot, except that they wore gold. Now the roaring was for the gold ones, and banners of gold and white broke out all over the place.

A hush fell, save for the all-pervading Voice of God. The people sat tense and silent, and it was plain that the real battle was about to begin. A few men on each side took their positions, and one of the balls was set down in the center, as if the battle was to be over that. Marya assumed that they would fight for possession of it; but suddenly it was kicked into the air, and the other side grabbed it and rushed forward with it.

Impossible to determine whether this was a battle or a game. At times it seemed that one side was trying to grab the ball and run away with it, while the other side was trying to stop them. They did it with incredible roughness, hurling themselves at one another; when one fell, the others flung themselves upon him with murderous fury. But suddenly they would all get up and start the same procedure again. Such behavior was bound to have ritual significance.

The same thing applied to the cheer-leaders. Obviously they must be playing the part of demons, or trying to invoke demons to take part in the battle. She was the more certain of this, because always above the uproar the Voice of God was speaking; she could not make out whether He was encouraging His side, or trying to frighten the enemy. Marya was used to having God tell His chosen people what to do; nor was she surprised that no one seemed to be heeding it. That had happened frequently in the history of the Hebrews.

The children of Galilee had a game which they played with a ball, a "kaddur." But it could never have occurred to Marya to compare that simple game with the fierce battering and ramming contest she now witnessed. What these trained gladiators did was evidently a matter of life and death to a hundred thousand men and women of the new world. Events on that field were the occasion for such frenzies of jubilation as stunned her senses. The crashing music of the band, the battle-songs, the volleys of cheering — all could be nothing but a process of incantation; she sensed around her the presence of Satan and his demons, Bar-Tit, Bar-Tema, Chashmagoz, Merigoz, and the rest; also the hosts of heaven, the cherubim, the seraphim, the choirs of the angels — even the All-Holy One, Rebono-shel-olam, Master of the Universe.

IN ARAMAIC

I

THE battle came to a halt, and the gladiators left the arena. However, the spectators stayed in their seats, and the visitor from Palestine sat patiently. There was nothing else for her to do.

The young woman in the white robe and the golden crown who sat on Marya's left had paid no attention to her, and continued to pay none. Possibly it was because she was a Gold, while Marya, by the symbol on her dress, was a Green. But the four black-clad gentlemen on her right were Greens, and they could not go on ignoring this strange dark woman who sat so silent through all the excitement, yet who wore the colors of their nation.

A boy came along, clad in white, with a little tray full of things to eat. The man nearest to Marya bought a bag of white, flaky grains; and after he had supplied himself and his friends, he turned to the stranger and said, "Will you have some?"

Marya realized that this was a courtesy; but she was a Jewish woman, and it was not permitted her to eat strange foods prepared by Gentile hands. For a moment she was taken aback; then in a low voice, she said: "Lo, riboni."

The effect of those words was surprising. The stranger stared at her; then he turned in his seat and looked steadily. "What did you say?" he demanded.

Marya could only shake her head and answer her usual, "Lo meyvin,"—"I do not understand."

When Marya had entered, this man had seen a thin, grey-haired woman in a peasant's costume; since there were all sorts of costumes about him, he had given no thought to her. But now he noted differences. It is one thing when a lady in a modern home takes a bath, and sits at her dressing-table and arranges her hair and complexion, and puts on a peasant robe, adding a touch of perfume and a jewel or two; but it is quite another thing when a real peasant woman tends her beasts in the pasture, hoes her vegetables and gathers some of them, cooks them on a wood fire outside her hut, and tramps over stony roads in worn and dusty sandals.

Meeting the gaze of the strange gentleman, Marya saw that he was about Jeshu's age, which was thirty. His face, unduly pale, was that of a student, and apparently a kind person. The black cloth of his costume was the finest she had ever beheld; the tight collar kept his head erect and made him seem trim and neat; the inner, white collar was hard and shiny beyond anything known to a woman who did her laundry by the side of a stream.

The name of this gentleman was Michael Henry O'Donnell, and he was a priest-professor of Semitic languages in Notre Dame University. He had devoted his studious life to acquiring certain special knowledge, and was one of the few persons of his Catholic Church who knew the Aramaic language — frequently but erroneously called Chaldee. If there was anything in the world that Father O'Donnell was sure of, it was that Aramaic had not been spoken as a living language for fifteen centuries or more. But here was a woman, apparently an uneducated peasant, who said: "Lo, riboni," that is, "No, my lord." Father O'Donnell searched his mind for any modern semitic language which might contain these words and the others Marya had used. He knew that there were so-called Chaldaic Christians who live near Mosul, and had been treated with great cruelty by the Turks during the World War. Could this gentle and anxious-looking woman be one of their peasant refugees?

II

NO MODERN scholar knows how the ancients pronounced any dead language. He can only make guesses, and the young priest now made them with Marya. Speaking slowly and carefully, he formulated a sentence: "Menan at atyah?"— that is, "Where do you come from?"

To the woman it was as if an angel had come from the sky. So lonely and anxious she had been — and now here was a friend! "Praise the Lord!" she exclaimed. "Our Father Our King!" Then she answered, "M'Gallil,"— "From Galilee." And she rushed on talking.

It was amazing to Father O'Donnell — the way she pronounced the gutterals, for example! A Westerner can hardly imagine how such sounds are made; they appear to come from underneath the throat, and remind one of the efforts of a mute person to make sounds.

"What town in Galilee?" asked the priest.

"Nazeret," said Marya.

The other took a few moments to think that over; then he asked, "When did you leave Nazareth?"

"Lo meyvin, riboni," answered Marya; which was quite true, for she had no idea when she left. She added: "It was at night"—which puzzled Father O'Donnell so that he asked her to repeat it. He was seeking to understand the peculiarities of her accent; he continued to speak slowly, using simple words, and she did the same.

"How did you come here?" was his next question.

Now Marya of course knew that she was in the future, and had, according to his ideas, no right to be there. So, to prepare his mind, she said: "Charshah," which means "Magic, enchantment." In Hebrew, it is "keeshoof"—such were the differences which told so much to the specialist in Semitic dialects, and at the same time threw his mind into chaos, since what they told him could not possibly be true!

"Charshah?" said Father O'Donnell, and looked at the stranger with sharp concern. She appeared innocent and good — but still, it does no harm to take precautions. He took one finger and made a motion on his breast — first from the top down, and then from side to side, at the same time murmuring: "In nomine Patris, Filii, et Spiritus Sancti." Marya, sharing his caution, said a formula of her own: "Shabriri-briri-riri-ri"— which is to say: "May it not be an evil eye."

Both of them waited; but nothing happened — except that the gigantic Voice was heard over the field again. Marya at last had a chance to find out about it. Pointing to the sky, she said: "Kol Shaddai?"— that is, "The Voice of the Terrible One?"

The priest knew what these words meant, but he did not get her idea. One cannot point to a Voice, but Marya waved her hands above her head and said: "Kolminshamaya?"—"The Voice from Heaven?" This was unmistakable Aramaic; in Hebrew she would have said: "Kol-mishamayim."

When the young priest understood that this peasant woman referred to the sound amplifier, he could not help smiling. He assured her that it was not the Lord who was speaking, and that it was not "charshah." When she pointed to the airplanes in the sky, he told her that Satan had no part in their performances. However, when she asked about the words printed on the tails of the planes, he was not so sure that she would agree; he did not translate to her the one which was just passing over them, which said: "Try Jigley's Gin."

The crowds started roaring again, the greens and the golds at the same time; the gladiators were running back onto the field. Marya now had a chance to find out what this was all about; she pointed, and said: "Karaba?"– that is, "battle?" The man smiled again, and said, "Lo! lo!" He wanted to tell her that it was a game, and wished he had his well-worn Hebrew-Chaldee dictionary with him. At last he was able to remember "mischak," which means laughter and also jest. Since this was not enough, he said, "riglah," which is "foot," and "kaddur," which is "ball."

"Riglah-kaddur-mischak," he repeated, and the grave, earnest woman repeated it after him; but it did not clear her mind. The gladiators had gone into action, and a moment later one of them was violently assaulted and knocked senseless; as stretcher-bearers came to carry him off the field, the woman asked, "Mischak?"

The priest smiled and said "Ken," which is "yes."

In the lull that followed he turned to the friend who sat next to him. "This woman speaks Aramaic, one of the dead languages."

Father Callahan had an honest Irish face, broad and jolly, and now red from much yelling. "Indeed?" said he; and then, suddenly: "They're putting in Zabriesky!" He sprang to his feet, along with a thousand other spectators. "Attaboy, Zabriesky!" he roared — and this was not a dead language.

III

FATHER Michael Henry O'Donnell was a conscientious priest and hard-working student, and this was the first real holiday he had allowed himself for some time. Also it was his first visit to California, an occasion to which he had looked forward for months. He and his three colleagues had travelled with the team, and all the way they had talked about this game. Last year the "Trojans," as the enemy team called themselves, had come from Los Angeles to South Bend and given the Irish a trouncing, and now the Irish were in Los Angeles, lusting for revenge. A tremendous occasion; and if anybody had told the young priest that at the supreme moment of the game he would be only half aware of it, he would have been willing to lay heavy odds against any such possibility.

The Golds had been driving down the field, approaching the double posts in front of Marya. Now suddenly they attempted a forward pass, and one of their gladiators broke through, and racing across the line, leaped high into the air and caught the ball and touched it to the ground. Pandemonium broke loose; the Golds rose as one man, and hands and handkerchiefs and hats went into the air. Down by the edge of the field the cheer-leaders were turning handsprings and back somersaults. The young woman at Marya's side cast dignity to the winds, and began dancing and shrieking in a fashion most bewildering to a visitor from ancient Palestine.

Marya looked at her, and then turned to the young priest — who remained seated and silent. "Mah?" said she, pointing to the young woman; that is, "Why?" she had to say it into his ear.

Father O'Donnell was somewhat at a loss to approach this explanation. He wanted to say that students at an American university had taken for play purposes the symbols of an ancient legend; the wooden horse, and the queen with a face that sank a thousand ships. He knew that the plains of windy Troy were not far from Galilee; but he didn't know if there was an Aramaic name for the town, and he doubted if Marya had ever heard of Homer. No, it was too much; he contented himself with saying: "Za malk'ta yavanit," which is to say: "This is a Greek queen."

Marya's worst impressions of Greek civilization were confirmed. She wished to move a little further away from this shrieking maenad; but the seats did not permit it — and anyhow, she had to remember that the four black-clad men were also "goyim" and they had recently been conducting themselves in the same undignified manner.

The priest felt that his explanation was scarcely adequate; and as it was some time before the game got under way again, he said into her ear that the Greek queen and all the other persons in costume, and likewise the players on the field, represented a place of learning, a school. Marya knew what a school was; it was called a "berab," and was a mud hut of the same size as her own, in which a dozen or so small boys sat on a bare floor, and scratched the fleas on their legs, and chanted Hebrew texts without understanding a word of them. She knew also about higher learning; for Sepphoris was what the Jews called a rabbinical center, and there was a "bet-ha-midrash," a place where men with long black beards gathered, and pored over ancient scrolls, and engaged in solemn but acrimonious controversies as to minute details of doctrine and ritual. But what was the connection between this and a "malk'ta yavanit" with a gold crown and sceptre? Or a hundred thousand people shrieking madly over a "riglah-kaddur-mischak," a football laughter or jest?

IV

NO, THE world of the future was not to be comprehended. But still, Marya clung to the faith that there must be some reason why Zar had brought her here. So she tried to find out everything she could. She took a fresh start, pointing to the green pasteboard flowers which had been pinned to her robe. Father O'Donnell was sure that even if he had had his Hebrew-Chaldee dictionary, he would not have found the word "shamrock," so he told her the English name, and she repeated obediently. He explained that there was a people called the Irish, who also had a "bet-ha-midrash," a place of learning. It was called Notre Dame, which meant Our Lady, in Aramaic "Ribanti;" it was a very holy name in the religion of the green people.

Of course Marya wanted to know about "Ribanti;" who was she, and what did she have to do with a place of learning? The football game had got started again, and the greens had the ball, and Father Callahan and the other priests were on their feet shouting loud demands that Zabriesky should "kill them," and that Danny Hogan should "eat them up," and that Rafferty should "ramble through them;" but the young priest felt obligated to answer Marya's questions, for it was his religion, and that stood first in his conscience — and he perceived that it was the same with this grave peasant woman from Palestine. She had made little effort to understand about football laughter or jest, but she wanted to know all about "Our Lady," who was an object of worship to the people of the future.

"She is a goddess, my lord?"

Father O'Donnell said no, she was the Mother of God, a woman who had brought God into the world.

"I understand," said the woman of Palestine. "It is in the Gentile religions. I have heard many such stories."

The good priest explained patiently. Our Lady, Ribanti, was a virgin; the greens called her the Blessed Virgin, the Queen of Heaven — "Malka-min-shamaya." God had come to her. It would have been embarrassing to explain this, if it had not been so holy. The Aramaic language is crude and explicit, but Father O'Donnell did his best to be tactful in making clear what had occurred.

"I understand," said Marya again. It was perfectly simple. The Greeks, the Romans, many other Gentiles had such stories. "But we Jews have nothing to do with them," she added. "We believe in One God, Abinushebashomayim — Our Father in Heaven."

Ever patient, the young priest affirmed that he too was a monotheist. There was One God only, but He manifested himself in three aspects, the Father, the Son, and the Holy Ghost. Father O'Donnell repeated all these words, and made sure that Marya understood them. A triune Godhead, three in One; the ever-blessed Trinity.

"Yes, yes!" replied the woman. "The Romans have it, but with them it is only two. They are building him a temple in Tibaryahu; my son, my first-born, has told me about it. There is a statue in front, and it has two faces, one this way and one in back"— Marya was showing with her hands how the statue of Janus looked, though she could not recall the name of this double one.

"It is not like that," said the kind father, wounded in soul.

And again Marya greed politely. "If it had three heads, it would have to be different," said she.

V

AT THIS time the "riglah-kaddur-mischak" was taking a turn in favor of the Greens. Zabriesky had killed two of his enemies, and Danny Hogan had at least partially eaten up another, and Rafferty had just rambled for fifteen or twenty yards. The other priests were on their feet waving green flags and bellowing like three bulls of Bashan; but Father O'Donnell sat in his seat, and in spite of proddings from his friends, was not to be diverted from his Aramaic conversation. He was no longer a young Irishman "rooting" for Notre Dame; he was a man exploring a volcano, and feeling the ground beginning to give way under his feet.

With gaze fixed upon the thin, worn face of this grandmother, he asked: "What is the name of the town you mentioned?"

"Tibaryahu," said Marya.

He repeated the name after her, bringing to bear his knowledge of Semitic language structure. "You do not know the Roman name?"

"No, riboni. I do not talk with the Romans."

"Is it a city they are building?"

"Yes, riboni."

"Do you know where it is?"

"B'gallil, riboni"— that is, "In Galilee, my lord." She added: "It is by the lake."

The explorer of the volcano got a whiff of sulphur smoke. He backed away, and got his breath, and finally put another question: "Do you know who is the Roman emperor?"

Marya shook her head. "I am a poor woman," she pleaded. "I am very ignorant."

"Would you know it if you heard it?"

"I am not sure."

"Is it Tiberius?"

A light broke upon her face. "Yes, riboni! I have heard it!"

"Then the name of the city is in honor of the emperor?"

"It may be so, riboni."

"Do you know the name of the procurator of Galilee?"

"He is Herod."

"Herod the father, or his son?"

"The son. He is called Herod Antipas. He is a very evil man."

The crust of the volcano broke, and Father O'Donnell felt himself sliding down into the crater. He gazed at Marya with such a look on his face that she was alarmed. "Have I done wrong to speak so of him, riboni?"

He sought to calm her mind. "I am interested in Galilee. I have studied about it. I would be grateful if you would answer more questions."

"Yes. Surely!"

"Tell me your name."

"I am called Marya."

"And your son? Your petach valda that you speak of?"

"He is named Jeshu." Then, since the priest continued to stare, she added: "The Romans call the name Iesu. You have heard that name?"

"I have heard that name," said Father O'Donnell. His voice had fallen low. "You have a husband?" he asked.

"My husband is dead."

"What was his name?"

"He was Josef, a carpenter."

"A carpenter of Nazareth—Nazaret b'Gallil?"

The young priest's voice was hardly audible.

"He was a good man, riboni."

"He was your husband from the beginning?"

"Surely, riboni. We Jewish women do not change husbands like the Gentiles."

"I mean — he was your husband before you had any children?"

"Ribono-shel-olam — the Lord of Heaven! I am a respectable woman."

"How many children have you, Marya?"

"I had nine; but the Lord has taken three."

"Tell me this: have you ever seen a malaach, an angel?"

"No, riboni! Who am I that angels would come to me?"

"You have never heard the voice of a malaach?"

"Never, my lord."

"You are just a good mother?"

"I have tried to be, my lord."

"And when your first-born came — did anything special happen?"

"I was very happy. I forgot my pain and rejoiced that a man had been born into the world."

Father O'Donnell's way of looking at Marya grew more and more strange. "Where did you hear those words?" he demanded, hastily.

"It is something that Jeshu says. He uses many beautiful words. It might be an angel when he speaks."

At this moment there was a mighty roaring of the crowd, and malk'ta yavanit, the Greek queen, the mad one, leaped to her feet and began to wave her flag, along with all the other Golds. Father Callahan turned to his colleague and caught him by the arm, crying in a voice of anguish: "We have lost the ball! And on their ten-yard line!"

Father O'Donnell pulled his arm away. "Let me be!" he exclaimed, impatiently.

"What's the matter with you, Mike?" cried Father Callahan. "Have you gone out of your wits?"

VI

THE young professor of Semitic languages, striving desperately to understand what was happening to him, suddenly recalled what Marya had told him, that she had come by "charshah." He crossed himself again as he asked her to tell him what the spell had been.

Said the peasant woman: "It was made by a sorceress, a woman from Nabataea. That is a hot land, and desert."

"What did this woman do?"

"She has a familiar spirit whose name is Zar. I asked that Zar should take me into the future; and then I fell into a swoon, and I was here. Is this the future, riboni?"

Father O'Donnell had never thought of it as the future, but he said: "It has been some nineteen hundred years since Herod Antipas was procurator of Galilee."

"So long as that, riboni? Then indeed it is a most wonderful charshah that the Nabataean has!"

"We do not have charshah nowadays, Marya, so it is hard for me to believe this tale of yours."

"It is all that I know, riboni. I am here, but I do not know why I am here, or what all this has to do with me. Nineteen hundred years! And what has happened? Have there been wars all that time?"

"Yes, Marya. But there has been a new religion, also."

"The one that tells about Our Lady, Ribanti? And about the son she bore when she was a virgin? And about the Three-headed God? I do not believe a word of it!"

"Hush, Marya!" said the young priest; he crossed himself again. "In nomine Patris, Filii, et Spiritus Sancti!" The woman from Palestine countered with her own spell: "Shabriri-briri-riri-ri."

As before, nothing happened; and at last the visitor to the future remarked: "Nineteen hundred years! So then Jeshu was mistaken! The world did not end so soon as he expected."

"Did Jeshu tell you that the world was going to end soon?"

"He insisted that it would end before we

passed away. Therefore we should not heap up treasures on earth, nor take thought saying what shall we eat or what shall we drink or wherewithal shall we be clothed; for our Heavenly Father, Abinu-shebashomayim, knoweth that we have need of these things."

Again Father O'Donnell was crossing himself; he did it almost every time he spoke now. "Tell me, Marya, how old is your first-born — I mean how old was he when you left Nazareth?"

"About thirty, riboni."

"Was he at home?"

"No, riboni. He had gone upon a journey. He told me that he must be about his Father's business. He had gone to the river Jordan."

"For what had be gone there?"

"To hear the preaching of Johanen, and perhaps to be dipped by him in the waters of the river. I was afraid that he might give offense to the Romans, and be crucified by them; so I went to the Nabataean woman and asked that her demon should take me into the future, that I might know what would become of my Jeshu, and of me. But I fear that Zar has made a mistake, for it is clear that all this has nothing to do with either of us."

Father O'Donnell came to a sudden decision.

"Marya," said he, "I wish you to meet some friends of mine. They may be able to tell you some of the things you wish to know. Will you come with me?"

"Surely, riboni," said she. Where else could she go?

The second quarter of the game ended, and the players ran off the field, and the spectators settled back to rest, and discuss the various plays, and eat peanuts and pop corn, and drink from little flasks which they carried, the gentlemen in hip-pockets and the ladies in hand-bags. Father O'Donnell leaned over to his friends and spoke. "Fellows, I have got to leave."

"What?" cried they. "In the middle of the game?"

"It has to do with this woman. I cannot explain here. It is a grave matter, concerning the welfare of the Church."

"The Blessed Virgin protect us!" exclaimed Father Callahan. He and his friends knew that O'Donnell had travelled two thousand miles to see this game, and if he had lost interest, it must indeed be a grave emergency. All they could do was to stare, while he rose and made his way to the nearest tunnel, followed by his odd-looking companion.

Chapter Five 117

AVE MARIA

I

FATHER Michael Henry O'Donnell put his charge into a taxicab, and said to the driver: "The Convent of Our Lady of the Sacred Heart." While they were moving with dizzy speed, he explained to the visitor a little of the charshah which caused chariots to behave in this manner. He listened to her exclamations over the immense size of the buildings, and when she said that they scraped the sky, he told her that this fact had been noted by others. She asked him the name of this far-spreading city, and he translated for her the ancient Spanish name so cherished by all real estate boosters: The City of Our Lady the Queen of the Angels.

"It is that Ribanti again?" asked Marya. "You name everything for her?"

"She is the object of our deepest devotion,"

said the young priest. "She intercedes for us with the Father."

Said Marya: "My first-born assures me that no intercession is needed. The Father knoweth what we have need of, and hears us when we speak."

They came to the Convent of Our Lady of the Sacred Heart; an elaborate structure, and Marya trembled to trust herself beneath such a weight of stone. But where her guide went, she followed, and found herself in a reception hall with a marble floor, and white walls, bare except for pictures. She gazed with curiosity, for she knew that this was a place of the religion of the Greens. There were pictures of a mother with a child in her arms, and she guessed that this was "Ribanti." She was a gentle and sweet-looking person, of some Gentile race which Marya could not identify.

The peasant from Galilee was extrmely hostile in her thinking about this woman who said that God had come to her and gotten her with child, and had made people believe her. Marya's Jahveh was a stern and serious Ruler of His universe; he did not go romping about the earth, consorting with virgins and getting them into trouble; on the contrary, He sat aloft in His heavenly mansion, wearing a long black beard and a snow-white robe, and every evening He read through the six tractates of the Mishnah. Marya knew this, because it was stated in one of the Talmudic texts which were written in her Aramaic language and read aloud in the synagogue.

There was another picture on the wall; a man hanging upon a cross, with a crown of thorns pressed on his head. The visitor wondered whether this cruel method of execution was still used by the people of these future days. The man had nails driven through both his hands and his feet, and she thought that these people had carried their torture further than the Romans, who, in their crucifying, nailed only the hands. Was this a warning to those who refused to bow before the Three-Headed One? Marya decided to be careful of her speech.

II

THERE came forward a woman in a black robe even more voluminous than Marya's and having an elaborately starched white hood. It was easy for Marya to guess that she was one of the priestesses of the Woman-God. Marya had a prejudice against the idea of women holding religious offices; a Gentile practice, invariably associated with sexual looseness.

Father O'Donnell introduced himself to the nun, and said that he wished to speak with the Mother Superior upon a very urgent matter. He and his charge were escorted into a little reception room, with more pictures of Ribanti and of crucified men. Presently came a stately lady with a grave face and a still more voluminous black robe and more elaborately starched linen. Father O'Donnell bowed and told who he was, and said, "I have just come from the game."

"Who won?" asked the Mother Superior.

"The Trojans were ahead when I left, but it was only half over. I felt obliged to leave, because I met this woman sitting next to me in the stadium, and what I learned from her seemed of grave importance to our Church."

"Indeed?" said the Mother, and glanced curiously at the grey-haired, dark woman, so eccentrically clad.

"It is so urgent that I am going at once to see your bishop, and put the matter into his keeping. Until he has decided what is to be done, I do not feel that I ought to discuss it with anyone. I wish to ask you to shelter this woman until I return with the bishop."

"Of course I wish to serve you, Father. But let me ask, is the woman dangerous?"

"She is a quiet and, I think, good person; but unless I am greatly mistaken, she is being made the tool of some who wish to harm our Holy Church. I feel that I am too inexperienced to cope with so grave a matter. I say this to impress upon you the importance of discretion. I beg you to keep the woman in your own apartment, and say nothing about her to anyone."

"The Blessed Virgin defend us!" exclaimed the Mother Superior. She looked at the stranger more closely, noting the obvious fact that she belonged to the lower classes. "I will do my best, of course. But naturally I am disturbed by what you tell me. What am I to say to this woman?"

"You will not be able to say anything to her, because she does not understand any —" Father O'Donnell was about to say "any modern language," but he checked himself and said "any language that is commonly spoken. I will explain to her she is to wait here. I am sure that she will make no trouble."

"Just what am I to do with her?"

"You might give her some devotional books with pictures in them."

"She is not of our faith?"

"Her beliefs, I am sorry to say, are quite hostile to ours. But she may be taught."

"Am I to give her anything to eat?"

"I am not sure that she will take it. She has ritual notions about food. I will ask her."

Father O'Donnell explained to Marya that he was going at once to bring the high priest of his Church, the "kahana rabbah," to talk with her; meanwhile he wished to leave her with this great lady of the Church, who was kind and would do everything for her. Unfortunately the lady did not know Aramaic. She wished to offer her food. Would Marya drink milk?

Marya answered that she might not drink milk that had been drawn by a Gentile. She might not eat the flesh of beasts which had been slaughtered by Gentile hands, nor bread which had been prepared by them. It was not easy to think of things which she might and would eat, but it was finally decided that the Mother Superior would provide for her strange and disturbing guest a plate of California walnuts and mission figs. The Mother Superior led her upstairs, praying to herself to have this odd-looking dark creature taken off her hands as quickly as possible.

III

THE taxi took Father O'Donnell to the home of Bishop Milligan. He learned that the bishop was at the game, so there was nothing to do but wait. The spiritual director of the City of Our Lady the Queen of the Angels proved to be a large, full-blooded gentleman, blessed with ability to carry the cares of a big business without interfering with his digestion. Now, however, there was sorrow on his brow. "A rout!" he exclaimed. "An utter catastrophe!"

It was several kinds of defeat for the Greens. The University of Southern California being a Protestant institution, it was a defeat for the true religion, a humiliation to Our Lady, the Queen of Heaven, Regina Angelorum. The Trojans being Greeks, while Notre Dame was Irish, it was also a national defeat. It might even be looked upon as a proletarian defeat; for the team of Our Lady was recruited from coal-heavers, iron-miners, steel-puddlers, stevedores, the huskiest products of the Irish and Polish and German Catholic populations in America; while the Trojans were the sons of ranch-owners and polo-players of the Anglo-Saxon elite. "And we didn't even score!" moaned Bishop Milligan, devoted son of the church, of Ireland, and of the working-class.

The priest explained that he had left before the game was over; a statement which called for immediate explanation. Said he: "Two things I must make clear to your excellency to begin with. I know what football customs are, and I want to assure you that I am entirely sober."

"All the Irish are sober now," said the bishop, a man of the world. "But some of them may drown their sorrows before night."

"I had a cocktail before lunch, and two glasses of wine at the end. That is more than I am used to, but the effect, whatever it may have been, has long since worn off."

"Really, Father! You don't have to trouble yourself about that!"

"I am doing it, because when you hear my story, you will probably be wishing to smell my breath. It is a most amazing thing."

"Pray proceed with the story."

"The other thing I have to explain is that I have specialized in ancient Semitic languages. I spent four years in the American College at Rome. I know not merely Old Testament Hebrew and all the rabbinic stuff; I know a bit of the East and the West Syrian dialects, and I know thoroughly the Aramaic which was spoken in ancient Galilee."

"A most unusual equipment, Father O'Donnell."

"I mention it, so that your excellency may realize that I know what has happened to me. Not many of our faith can understand these incidents as I do, and for that reason they may be inclined to distrust my story, and think that I am temporarily out of my mind."

"Really, my dear Father, I cannot imagine myself forming such an opinion of a professor of Notre Dame! Pray trust me to hear you seriously."

IV

FATHER Michael Henry O'Donnell began his story back in South Bend, Indiana, a safe and sane if dingy industrial city. He told how he and his colleagues had looked forward to this excursion; he was still young — nor was his excellency, the bishop, too old to sympathize. He told how the four members of the faculty had travelled with the team; being treated as guests of honor, and put into an open car and driven around the field with the floats.

"I saw you," said the bishop.

"We were seated among those who had been riding on the floats. They wore many kinds of costumes, so I paid no attention when I found myself next to a woman in a peasant's robe and rough sandals. In the intermission I spoke to her. You understand, your excellency, she is a respectable-appearing person; she must be close to fifty, and says she is a grandmother; she sat alone, and quite silent, so I thought it was the part of courtesy to address her."

"Quite so, Father."

"To my consternation she answered in the Aramaic language, which, as you know, has not been a living language for more than fifteen hundred years."

"Most curious!"

"I engaged her in conversation, seeking to learn what I could, and I made certain that she speaks the Galilean Aramaic of the time of Our Lord. She tells me that she lives in the village of Nazareth, and that her name is Marya — that is Mary — and that her husband's name was Josef, and that he was a carpenter; also that the Roman ruler of her province is named Herod Antipas."

"Really!" exclaimed the bishop. He did not know how to look — whether grave, like his visitor, or amused, as he wanted to. "Has it occurred to you that some one may be making you the victim of a hoax in very bad taste?"

"I did not fail to think of that, your excellency. But persons of the sort who would plan such a hoax would not be apt to possess the knowledge necessary to carry it out; and furthermore the actress who could play such a part would hardly be able to meet the tests to which I have subjected this woman."

Biship Milligan lost his impulse to smile; and the other went on: "The reason I have brought the matter to you, your excellency, is that the hoax, if it be one, must have been prepared by an enemy of our Holy Church — and one of truly diabolical cunning."

"You astound me, Father O'Donnell. Pray proceed!"

"I will repeat as briefly as I can what this woman says. It is difficult for me to utter the words; I beg you to bear in mind that they are not mine, but hers, which I have patiently drawn from her, after getting used to the peculiarities of her pronunciation."

"I beg you, Father. Speak freely!"

"The woman maintains that her name is Marya, and that her first-born son is named Jeshu, which the Romans call Iesu. She says that she has borne nine children, and had lived with her husband in the normal way when her first son was conceived. She says that no angel came to her, and she has never had any supernatural experience. She manifests great antagonism to the idea of a virgin birth, and of a Son of God coming to men; to her it is a Greek or Roman notion, and she has the strict monotheism of the Jews. She says that her son Jeshu is a carpenter, and that when she left Galilee, he was thirty years of age, and had gone to the river Jordan to hear the preaching of Johanen, that is John, and perhaps to be baptized by him."

"How truly horrifying!" exclaimed the bishop. What is your interpretation of all this?"

"I have none. I brought the problem to you, because I perceived that if this woman's tale were to become known, it would excite most odious mockery of our faith."

"That is clear, and you did well to come. Where is the woman?"

"I have placed her at the Convent of Our Lady of the Sacred Heart. The Mother Superior has promised to mention the matter to no one until she hears from you."

"You have been most discreet, Father O'Donnell. It is, as you say, a plot, not against yourself, but against the Holy Church. Does the woman herself understand what she is doing?"

"I fear you will find this hard to credit, until you have actually met her. She is, to all appearances, a good and kind person; very simple —

in short, just what she purports to be, a peasant woman of ancient Galilee. I could tell you a hundred details upon which I have tested her; she seems impervious to all attacks. Nor is it as if she were a cautious and reticent person; she answers quickly, and with vigor. The Galileans were notorious for being hot-blooded and impulsive."

More and more, as the learned priest spoke, the bishop realized the seriousness of the problem. Said he: "How does this woman say that she came here?"

"She says that it is sorcery."

"What?"

"She went to a soothsayer, a woman of Nabataea — it was part of ancient Arabia. She paid this sorceress to perform a spell, whereby a Nabataean demon was to carry her into the future, so that she might see what was going to happen to herself and to her first-born son. Then she swooned, and when she opened her eyes, she was outside our stadium, watching the crowds going into the game."

The two men were staring at each other. "Do you believe that, Father?" demanded the bishop.

"I do not know what to believe. We are

pleased to think of ourselves as modern men, and to say that demons are out of date. But we must bear in mind that our Church teaches that there are demons, and provides a ceremony for their exorcism, and makes it canonically available for all priests."

"That is unquestionable, Father."

"We are not obligated to believe that this woman is an energumen, but we are obligated to believe that she *may* be one."

"Quite so," said the bishop, submissively. He added: "Have you thought of the possibility that she may have been hypnotized?"

"Abnormal psychology is not my subject, and I do not know what modern psychical researchers may have discovered, or what powers they may have developed. I suppose it is conceivable that some one among them might cherish a furious enmity to our Holy Church, and might have hypnotized a woman, and taught her the Galilean Aramaic, and made her think herself the widow of a carpenter of Nazareth. But I am sure that he would have had to spend many years training the mind which I have been investigating. The task would seem to me so complicated, that if I were asked whether I would prefer to believe that a man has done this, or a demon, I would say, with our Blessed Savior: 'Retro me, Satanas.' "

"Your arguments are compelling, Father. Take me at once to this woman."

"One moment, your excellency. I know that you are a busy administrator, whereas I, a young student, have had time to devote to ancient learning. It occurs to me that possibly you do not know these Semitic languages."

"Frankly, Father, I don't know a word of them."

"Then you will be forced to rely upon my statements as to what the woman is saying."

"I have full confidence in that."

"It is too heavy a responsibility for me. There come times when I doubt the evidence of my own ears. It would be a great comfort to me if we could call in some reliable person who will be able to check at least a part of her talk."

The bishop thought for a moment: "We have a teacher of semitics at our Catholic university, Professor Case. He is a son of our Church, and I am sure can be trusted."

V

MARYA sat in a little room, with wonderfully smooth and clean white walls. In one corner was a little cot, and at its foot a table, and one chair in which she sat. Night had fallen, but the room was like day, because of a light which must be "charshah"— it had suddenly appeared, without even the saying of a spell. On the table were the remains of her supply of walnuts and figs; also several little books with pictures.

For an hour or two she had been studying these books. One was called "Under Mary's Mantle," and another "Our Mother of Sorrows," and another "Rosary Novenas to Our Lady." Marya, of course, could not read any of the titles, but the illustrations were almost is expressive. She knew that they must be pictures of Ribanti.

On the cover of one book was the Holy One, clad in a voluminous robe and a huge mantle, spreading the mantle so that it formed a sort of niche around her and under her feet. Within this shelter were gathered a number of persons easy to identify; a king with a crown, a high prelate, a learned doctor, a student with a book, a number of women and children, all kneeling in adoration. Ribanti herself wore a crown—she was the "malka minshamaya." Over her were five little baby heads with wings coming out of their necks, and it was not difficult for Marya to guess that these were cherubim.

Inside this little book were all sorts of stories about the Queen of Heaven, and the miracles she had wrought, and the mercies she had shown. The words which Marya was unable to read were such as these:

"O most beautiful flower of Mount Carmel! fruitful vine, splendor of heaven, singular bringer-forth of the Son of God still remaining a Virgin, assist me in this my necessity! O star of the sea, help me and show me herein that thou art my Mother! O holy Mary, Mother of God, Empress of heaven and earth, I humbly beseech thee from the bottom of my heart to succor me in this necessity; there are none that can withstand thy power."

There was a picture, showing the Empress of heaven and earth standing erect in a pose of command and holding out a sceptre of power; thre was a big crown on her head and about it a circle of light. In her other arm she held the little son of God, and He too had a light about His head, and in His hand a round ball. Marya did not know that the earth was round, so she missed the symbolism of that; but she saw on each side of the throne a choir of angels with great spreading wings, and lutes in their hands and songs on their lips; kneeling in front of them, facing the throne, were a company of kings, great warriors with their drawn swords laid flat, merchants, even peasant people like herself. Yes, there could be no question but that Ribanti had attained tremendous power in this world.

There were hundreds of such pictures for her to look at. The only trouble was that each mother appeared to be a different woman, and each son a different baby. Marya was shocked; the Greens had an evil and polygamous god! But presently her quick mind came to the idea that perhaps they had forgotten what their Queen of Heaven looked like, and had to paint her at a guess. Marya's artistic self was aroused, and she tried to decide which Ribanti she herself preferred; she finally chose one who was young and innocent-looking, having no baby. There was an angel standing by her side, and something written underneath. The prayer which Marya could not read began as follows:

"Sweet Mother Mary, meditating on the Mystery of the Annunciation, when the Angel Gabriel appeared to thee with the tidings that thou wert to become the Mother of God; greeting thee with that sublime salutation, 'Hail, full of grace! the Lord is with thee!' and thou didst humbly submit thyself to the will of the Father, responding: 'Behold the handmaid of the Lord. Be it done unto me according to thy word.' "

The door opened, and a black-clad nun stood in the doorway, signing Marya to come with her.

Chapter Six 141

SALVE REGINA

I

THREE black-clad gentlemen were sitting in the study of the Mother Superior when the nun brought Marya in. One was Father O'Donnell, and the other two were older men of gravity and authority. Both the newcomers wore strange devices set upon their noses, which made round circles about their eyes, and gave them the aspect of great owls. Marya understood that these must be magic circles, to protect them from unholy sights. "May it not be an evil eye!" she whispered to herself.

The nun retired and closed the door, and Father O'Donnell led Marya to a seat, and told her that these gentlemen were friends of his; one a high official of his church, and the other a scholar who understood her language. Marya's anxious face lighted up, and she expressed her pleasure to the learned one, who was pale, bowed, and wrinkled, as became a student. She addressed him as "Rabboni," that is to say, "my teacher." The bishop she addressed more ceremoniously as "kahana rabbah," that is, "high priest." He was big, and evidently a man of power, and she noted that the others were translating her words to him, and awaiting his comments.

They were polite to her as Father O'Donnell had been, and she decided that all people in this future world were kind — except when it came to football laughter or jest. Father O'Donnell explained that they were deeply interested in learning about the past of the world, and they hoped she would do them the favor to answer their questions. She promised to do her best. Her kind features revealed her sincere intent.

The young priest led the conversation. He had discovered that Professor Case did not possess much knowledge of Aramaic dialects, and he sheltered the gentleman by explaining that Marya's pronunciation was different from what scholars were used to. He was careful to spell out new words and translate them to both the professor and the bishop, and the professor invariably agreed that O'Donnell's version was correct. In that way they got along slowly but surely.

The bishop made it his affair to study the woman's face. It was weather-beaten, deeply lined — obviously a peasant face. He watched her changes of expression and tones of voice, to satisfy himself as to her honesty. Was she really of the ancient world, and was her ignorance of the modern world genuine? Was she a vicious plotter against the Holy Church, or a victim of such plotters — or had it now befallen Bishop Milligan of the City of Our Lady the Queen of the Angels, as it had befallen numerous other prelates throughout the glorious history of the Church, to be confronted by a genuine case of demonic possession?

"You know, Marya," Father O'Donnell was explaining, "we have never before met anyone from what is to us the past. We have books which tell us about those times, and we wish to see if what you know agrees with them."

"I will do my best to oblige you," she replied; "but remember that I am a poor and ignorant woman."

II

FATHER O'Donnell asked her to tell them some familiar things about Galilee. "Tell us about Tibaryahu. You have never been there yourself?"

"No, riboni. But I have seen Sepphoris; and I have seen the stones which the Romans carry for the building of Tibaryahu."

"Tell us about that."

So Marya launched upon an account of ancient methods of transportation and construction. She had seen the procession of four-wheeled carts, drawn each by a score of great oxen, which passed over the Via Maris, laden with white pillars of marble. The Romans made these somewhere, by the labor of slaves, she had been told. They brought whole cities into Galilee. She thought it was wasteful when buildings had so many white pillars, all exactly alike.

She used a phrase which Father O'Donnell could only translate by the words "mass production." She said that they carved endless images of their Gentile gods, including the two-headed one. They had women gods also, queens of heaven, and these queens bore sons of God. She wanted to say, "like Ribanti," but she remembered her resolve to check her tongue.

She did say that the "tzalmanah," that is, images, were forbidden to the Jews by their Torah, and she mentioned that her sons had learned to say those commandments in Hebrew, but she was not sure if she could repeat them. "Are those commandments in your books?" she asked; and she recalled: "Thou shalt not make unto thee any graven image, or any likeness of any thing that is in heaven above, or that is in the earth beneath, or that is in the water under the earth . . . "

They began to ask about her childhood. Yes, she knew who had ruled in Israel at that time; Herod, that was called the Great, but she knew not why, save for the greatness of his evil. She had heard some of the scandals of the court in those days; she hesitated to repeat them to strange gentlemen, but they assured her that it was history, and they had it in the books, so she told them, and they said it agreed with the books completely.

They asked her if she had even been to the place she called "Jerushalim," and she said they went up to the feasts, and she told about the temple which Herod had restored. It was a grand lot of buildings, but her Jeshu had been unhappy there, and refused to go any more; he said the priests spent their time arguing about subtleties of doctrine, and forgot justice and love, the spirit of the Law. The Jews who had become rich looked with scorn upon poor village people from Galilee; they called them "amme-ha-'aretz," and told stories about them to make them ridiculous.

"Do you remember any of these stories?" asked Professor Case.

"Yes," said Marya, and told about a gentleman who ordered his Galilean servant to boil him two feet of an animal; and because of the way the words were mispronounced in Galilee, she boiled him two lentils. Said Marya: "We people of the soil may say our words wrong, but we are far from being the clods they call us. In Sepphoris we have a priest-center, and many learned men."

"Ask her about that," said the bishop.

"The priest courses go up to Jerushalim to render service in the temple. They gather at Sepphoris and travel together; they wear robes according to their offices, and always beards — it would be impossible for us to understand that a kahana should be shaven, as you gentlemen are. The council of our elders all have beards reaching to their waists; the hazzan of the synagogue has one which he can tie about his waist."

Said the bishop: "Ask her if she has ever been to Egypt."

"No, riboni," replied Marya, in some surprise. "How should poor people travel to a land as far as Egypt?"

It was a temptation to Father O'Donnell to say: "Our books say that you did." But he bridled his tongue, for the three of them had agreed that no word should be said to give Marya any hint of what she meant or might seem to mean in their religion. To do so might enable her to do great harm to the Holy Church.

"Ask her if she has even been in Bethlehem," said the bishop.

She said: "I think I have heard of it, but I have never been there. Is that place in your books?"

"There is a prophecy of Micah," explained Father O'Donnell, "that the Messiah, the Annointed One, shall be born there."

"Is that so?" replied the woman. "Has he been born yet?"

"There is a dispute about it," said the young priest, and passed on hastily. "You have lived in Nazareth all your married life, Marya? All your nine children were born there?"

"Yes, riboni."

"You are sure of that?"

"Who should know better than I?"

There was a silence, during which she sat gazing from one to another. She sensed that they were disturbed about something; they were not good actors.

At last her friend asked her to tell them about her home, and what was her daily life. After she had mentioned many details of a humble, everyday sort, the kahana rabbah began proposing questions about her first-born. What did he look like? How far had he traveled? What books had he read? Did he know Hebrew? Did he know any Greek? How early had he begun to show his powers of thought?

"Very early," said the mother, proud to talk about her wonderful one. "As a little boy, when we went up to the temple, he was left behind, and we found him talking with the learned doctors. They were amazed at the knowledge he showed. He has never been as other men; he is so gentle and kind. And yet he can be angry, too; when he sees cruelty and injustice, a fury seizes him. That is why I fear for him; he is too good for our evil world."

III

THEY asked many more questions, and Marya answered from her heart, as always. Until at last Bishop Milligan leaned back in his chair and said: "I have heard enough. I am satisfied."

"I also," said Professor Case.

"I was satisfied before I came," said Father O'Donnell.

The bishop summoned a nun, and Marya was returned to her cubicle with the nuts and fruits and picture-books of Our Lady the Queen of the Angels.

"Well," said Father O'Donnell, to the others, "what is your verdict?"

"The woman is a peasant from Galilee." This from the bishop. "No man in his senses can doubt that."

"I agree," declared Case.

"And therefore, it cannot be questioned that she is an energumen."

"It cannot be questioned," echoed Case.

"The only problem is, whether this demon which possesses her is what she thinks, a Nabataean by the name of Zar, or whether it is Satan himself, in a perfidious endeavor to wreck the foundations of our Holy Church."

"Is it not possible that it may be both?" inquired Father O'Donnell.

"Perfectly so; the woman may be possessed by all the devils of hell. The fact that she is so innocent in appearance, and good in and of herself, may serve to render her the fit instrument of this conspiracy of the powers of darkness."

"Wisely spoken," said Case.

"The questions we now have to decide are practical ones." The bishop was an administrator, accustomed to getting things done. "I take it we are agreed that this conspiracy must be thwarted — with the help of the Blessed Virgin and the saints."

The others agreed. They approved everything the wise and capable prelate had to say.

Under no circumstances was this story to reach the outside world. The fact that Marya understood no word of any modern language made the secret theirs alone; it was a providential device for the overthrowing of an infernal intrigue. "I take it that no one of us three is going to indulge in the pleasure of gossiping about this grave matter."

"Not I," said Case.

"Nor I," said O'Donnell.

"In view of the gravity of the emergency, it appears to me proper that we should distrust the frailties of our mortal nature, and should call upon the aid of higher powers. I propose that the three of us shall take a vow."

The bishop arose in his authority ,and pronounced a solemn oath, that never while they lived would they permit any word about this woman to pass their lips, at any time, in any place, in any language — the bishop added everything he could think of, he called in all the heavenly host to guard and protect them in the keeping of a most holy compact. When they had raised their right hands and sworn, their spiritual ruler went on to pronounce a solemn anathema upon any one who should break this vow; he cursed that infirm one on earth and in hell, he delivered him to the fury of all the demons, he consigned him to eternal torments, now and forever, in saecula saeculorum, world without end, Amen.

IV

"AND now," said the bishop, "what is the next thing for us to do?"

"It seems to me evident," replied Father O'Donnell, "that we must proceed to exorcise this demon."

"Quite so," agreed Professor Case.

"Has either of you ever had any experience with exorcism?"

There was a silence.

"I must admit that it is new to me also," declared the bishop.

"But the Holy Church has made it easy for us," said the young priest.

"Everything has been provided for," added Case.

"We will follow the ritual and do our best," declared Milligan. "In the event that we do not succeed, and this woman still clings to the delusion that she is — what the demons have caused her to claim to be — why then, I take it that it will be necessary for us to have her incarcerated in an asylum. I am sure there will be no medical difficulty in establishing the incompetence of a woman who claims to have come from Palestine of the year thirty of Our Lord."

"Quite so," said the professor.

"If your excellency will pardon a suggestion ——" ventured O'Donnell.

"Yes, Father?"

"I would question whether this is the best mood in which to approach the ceremony of exorcism. It is necessary to bear in mind that the demons may be hearing every word we say; and is it wise to give them the suggestion that we ourselves do not trust the wisdom of the Holy Church, and the heavenly powers which we are authorized to invoke on behalf of this sorely distressed woman?"

"Father O'Donnell, you are correct. My words were those of a frail and mortal man, and not of a prelate of the Church and a deputy of Our Lord. With His help we shall make this ceremony effective, and cast these evil creatures forth, and save the soul of his worthy woman."

"With the help of the Father," said Case.

"And of the Son, and of the Holy Ghost," said O'Donnell.

"And of the Blessed Virgin and all the saints," added the bishop.

All three of them crossed themselves.

"What is your next suggestion?" asked Milligan — he was not going to make any more missteps!

"Let me mention, your reverence," said O'Donnell, "we had recently in the Religious Bulletin of our university the story of a very extraordinary case of an energumen from whom a host of demons were exorcised. I remember all the details, which were truly startling. The exorcist was a Capuchin friar from a monastery in Wisconsin, and the ceremony took place in a Franciscan convent in Iowa. The unfortunate woman was bound by nuns and placed upon a bed; but when the exorcist began his work, the possessed woman tore herself free from her bonds and from those who were trying to restrain her; her body was borne swiftly through the air and landed high above the door of the room, to which she clung with catlike grips."

"The heavenly powers defend us!" exclaimed Bishop Milligan.

"I too have heard of such incidents," said Professor Case. "The demons have infernal strength, and it is by no means easy to break their hold upon one of their victims."

"In this case at Earling, Iowa," O'Donnell went on, "it was necessary to carry on the work in strict privacy, because the demons shouted obscene statements concerning the private lives of the nuns and priests who took part in the exorcism."

"Dominus nobiscum!" exclaimed the bishop, and gazed about the room uneasily.

"By special dispensation, the exorcist wore a pyx containing the blessed sacrament; the energumen emitted excrements which were obviously preternatural in their volume and filth, and the demons hurled these at the pyx, but never successfully, of course."

"You think we have to prepare for such things here?"

"I should say we have to prepare for anything, your excellency — except for giving way to the demons and letting them retain possession of this woman's soul."

The bishop perceived that he had a resolute son of the Church before him, one who spoke with the fervor of true faith. It was the sublime fortune of the Church to raise up such in every generation. "Father O'Donnell," said he, "would it be possible for you to take charge of this ceremony?"

"I don't see how it can be, your excellency; I have my duties at the university. In the Iowa case, of which I am telling you, the siege of the demons lasted twenty-three days."

"Can it be possible?"

"I doubt not the exorcist was miraculously sustained; and of course he had a staff of priests and nuns to support him."

"I fear my episcopal duties will not permit me to undertake such a campaign as that. But you, Father O'Donnell, seem to have especial influence with this woman; and I am sure that I could persuade the authorities of the university to lend you to us for this important purpose."

"I am deeply interested in saving this good woman's soul," said the young priest. "If your excellency will make the arrangement, and will ask the blessings of heaven upon the undertaking, I will put myself humbly in your hands."

Chapter Seven

RETRO ME, SATANAS

I

NEXT morning a hanger-on at the delivery entrance of the Convent of Our Lady of the Sacred Heart might have seen an unusual spectacle, a she-goat being unloaded from a truck. Its hinder parts were neatly wrapped in cloths, so that it might not commit any indiscretion, and thus chastely garbed, it was led to the elevator and taken to the cubicle in which Marya had spent the night.

The peasant mother was of course delighted by this visitor, a reminder of home. Her dark and careworn face lighted up. She needed no more than a sign to suggest that she was to draw the creature's milk into a pail; she carefully washed her hands, according to ritual, and after that she no longer had to exist upon nuts and fruits. Surely these people of the future were kind!

Later in the day came Father O'Donnell, and a nun escorted her to a reception room to confer with him. Gently and tactfully he told her the decision to which he and the kahana rabbah and rabboni had come; they had investigated the demon Zar which had taken possession of her, and learned that he was a dreadful and perfidious monster, and that her soul was in the gravest peril.

Marya, was, of course, much frightened. "Ayah!" she wailed. "I have committed a great sin. What is to be done?"

The priest explained that his religion provided for the casting out of demons, and that these measures could be relied upon, because of the all-powerful nature of the heavenly ones who would support the effort.

"Is it Ribanti who will cast them out?"

"Ribanti will intercede with the Father, and He will do it."

"The Three-Headed One, riboni?"

The young priest assented, there being no time for controversy. The bishop had telephoned to Notre Dame, and obtained permission for O'Donnell to remain and perform this service for the Church. The bishop had ordered a corps of priests to support him, and the Mother

Superior had mobilized her nuns and placed a suitable apartment at the disposal of the operators. There was, needless to say, great excitement in the Convent of Our Lady of the Sacred Heart that morning. A woman who had spent the night with them was discovered to be possessed of a demon, and a band of hard-working California nuns were suddenly called upon to be witnesses of a miracle! Sancta virgine, ora pro nobis!

"But riboni," objected Marya, "is it right that I, at Hebrew woman, should be healed by Gentile spells?"

"You have been made ill by them, Marya; and surely you will pay us the compliment to assume that our ritual is no worse than that of a Nabataean sorceress."

Marya was in the hands of these Green people. She remembered her habits of submission. "I suppose that is true. I sinned against the Law when I went to that woman."

"You are in a most dangerous position, Marya. Your immortal soul may be at stake."

"Have I an immortal soul, riboni?"

"Surely you must know that you have one!"

"Only the Pharisees teach that, and those who

believe it wear fringes. Do any of the priests of Ribanti wear fringes?"

"You will see fringes shortly, for I am going to take you to the chapel where we shall perform a high mass for the salvation of your soul. I must explain to you about that. It is a most solemn ceremony, which may terrify the demon Zar and others he has brought with him, and cause them to leave you at once. I must explain the procedure — we take bread and wine, and turn it into the body and blood of our Lord,and then we eat it and drink it."

The woman gazed at him in dismay. "You eat and drink the body and blood of your God?"

"It is because He died for us, and He told us to do it, so that we might remember Him."

"Ai, ayah!" exclaimed the visitor from Palestine. "That is the most shocking idea I have heard in all the religions of the Gentiles!"

"Hush woman!" exclaimed the priest, sternly. "You do not know what you are saying! It is demon Zar who is speaking with your lips!"

II

FOUR nuns, sturdy in body and likewise in faith, constituted the guard which the Mother Superior had appointed for this duel with the demon. They marched Marya to the chapel, one leading the way, one close at each side, and one behind. It was not difficult for her to imagine that she was a prisoner.

Meanwhile, Father O'Donnell and two other priests were putting on their violet surplices; loose and flowing vestments with great wide sleeves and much lace. Over these they put the stoles, long strips that went around the back of the neck and hung down on each side over the breast. In the center of the stole was a cross, and each man kissed it before putting it on; it was "the yoke of the Lord." Each end of the stole had fringes.

Never before in Marya's life had she entered a place of worship of the Gentiles. The word conveyed to her all the evil which the word "heathen" conveys to the Christian, and throughout her pious life she had avoided every contact with Gentile affairs. Now she was led up to the front pew of the chapel, and confronted with this most awful of their rites. Before her was the jewelled and shining altar, and behind and above it hung the tortured Son of God with the crown of thorns upon his brow. She knew they were going to eat Him, and a shuddering seized her.

The organ sounded, and three priests marched solemnly forth; also two boys, one of them swinging a censer. He swung it directly at Marya, and a jet of grey smoke shot toward her, and the chapel became filled with a sweet pungent odor. The priests were chanting; once or twice she recognized a word, and knew that they were using the language of the Romans; she was confirmed in her impression that Ribanti was one of the maidens whom Father Jupiter had visited. Marya did what she could to protect herself; continually her lips whispered: "Rebono-shel-olam," that is, "Master of the Universe," and "Yit-gadal-vi'-yitgadashshmei-rabbo," or "Magnified and sanctified be His holy Name."

Bells rang, and she sat staring, as Father O'Donnell raised the host to his lips and put it into his mouth. Also he drank the wine, which his rites had mystically changed into blood. Marya waited for this strong magic to have effect upon her, but nothing happened so far as she could tell. She supposed that the spell was to cast out Zar; she could not guess that it was intended to make her give up the idea that she was the widow of Josef, and the mother of Jeshu, a grandmother and no virgin. She continued in her firm assurance that these priests and nuns were seekers after false gods, and that Shaddai, the Terrible One, was the true and only God.

III

THEY took her to a large room which had been equipped with a bed and some chairs, and an image of Ribanti and one of the man on the cross; also various objects such as basins and receptacles, and a strait-jacket.

They seated her on the edge of the bed, where she could fall without hurting herself. The four nuns sat in a row, perhaps ten feet away, ready to leap into action. In addition to the three priests, there were present Professor Case, and a priest-professor whom he had brought, one who understood the Arabic dialects; for it might be necessary to hold converse with Zar and his imps, to shame and blast them in their own tongue.

Father O'Donnell took his stand directly in front of Marya. No more was he the kindly person who had chatted with her at the football laughter or jest. He had prayed most of the night, and wrought himself to a state of white-hot fervor. He was the voice of his Holy Trinity, and of all the hosts of heaven, dominating and commanding the legions of hell. "Pater noster, qui est in coelo," he began, in his rolling Latin chant; and Marya whispered over and over: "Abinu-shebashomayim," which is ancient Hebrew for "Our Father in Heaven."

No one of the persons in this room had ever before witnessed the casting out of a demon. But the Holy Catholic Church is old, and has experienced everything, and provided for everything and all that one has to do is to follow the ritual. Father O'Donnell had studied and mastered it, and the other participants were borne along in the strong current of his faith.

The ceremony which he used had been made canonical by Pope Paul V, more than three hundred years ago. It began with the fifty-third Psalm, which is full of commination. "God hath scattered the bones of him that encamped against thee." At every sentence he made the sign of the cross over Marya; her forehead, her breast, the top of her head. She began to tremble violently, for she knew that this was powerful magic, and had no idea what it might do. The last shot of charshah had carried her nineteen hundred years into the future; the next one might rend her apart, or turn her into an ape or a jackal. She stared at the exorcist with the fixity of a hypnotized rabbit at a snake; the faces of the nuns bore much the same expressions; while as for the priests and professors, they maintained their dignity, and put their trust in their Holy Church.

Lest any doubts might assail them, the exorcist read from the tenth chapter of St Luke, in which their Master gave to his followers specific authority to do this thing:

"And the seventy returned again with joy, saying, Lord, even the devils are subject unto us through thy name.

"And he said unto them, I beheld Satan as lightning fall from heaven.

"Behold, I give unto you power to tread on serpents and scorpions, and over all the power of the enemy: and nothing shall by any means hurt you."

Armed with such divine sanction, Father O'Donnell hurled himself upon the demon. "I command you, whoever you may be, foul spirit, and all your companions who have taken possession of this servant of God." In glorious old Latin words he summoned the heavenly powers: "Domine sancte, Pater omnipotens, aeterne Deus, Pater Domini nostri Iesu Christi." He invoked all the holy mysteries: "Per mysteria Incarnationis, Passionis, Resurrectionis, et Ascensionis Domini nostri Iesu Christi." He commanded the demon to tell his name, and the day and hour he would leave, and to give a sign.

But the demon gave no sign. Marya continued to stare and be badly scared; but that was all. The exorcist began to pour abuse upon the stubborn devil, baiting him into utterance. He reminded him how God had thrown him out of heaven. He called him a whole string of opprobrious names—"enemy of the faith, foe of the human race, bringer of death, thief of life, denier of justice, root of evil, spreader of vices, seducer of men, betrayer of nations, exciter of envy, origin of avarice, cause of discord, exciter of griefs;" all this in the grave canonical tongue. "Retire therefore! Give place to the Holy Spirit!"

Those who had composed these ancient incantations had known the nature not merely of demons, but also of exorcists. Father O'Donnell made it plain to the "old serpent" that he was not to be permitted to evade because of any weakness of Father O'Donnell himself. "Yield, therefore, not to me, but to the minister of Christ . . . Stay not on account of my sins . . . I abjure you again, not by my infirmity, but by the virtue of the Holy Spirit, that you go out from this servant, Marya, whom an All-powerful God has made in his image."

IV

FROM the literary point of view it was a grandiloquent composition; while from the point of view of psychology it was a masterpiece of the technique of suggestion. Tirelessly the exorcist poured abuse upon the evil one; again and again he bade him come forth, in the name and by the authority of the most awful holy majesties. "Go out, transgressor! Go out, seducer, full of all grief and falsehood, enemy of virtue, persecutor of the innocent! Most evil dragon, He commands thee, born of a virgin! Jesus of Nazareth commands thee! Go out, impious one! Go out, scoundrel! Go out with all your betrayals! Hell is your place, the serpent is your habitation!"

But still the demon stayed. The exorcist read from St Luke the canticle sung by Mary when the angel revealed to her that a virgin was to bear a child to the Lord. "For He that is mighty hath done to me great things; and holy is his name." When this had no effect, the exorcist recited the sixty-seventh Psalm, full of fears and questionings, but ending in triumphant confidence: "I will remember the works of the Lord; surely I will remember thy wonders of old."

This about concluded the ancient ceremony; but Father O'Donnell had no idea of giving up. He had read up on demons, and knew their stubbornness, and had made a vow not to accept even a temporary defeat. Tirelessly making the sign of the cross, he recited prayers to the Blessed Virgin, Queen of Heaven, Our Lady of the Sacred Heart, Notre Dame des Douleurs, Nuestra Señora la Reina de los Angeles. Just as he had formerly called the demon bad names, he now called the Virgin good ones:

"Queen of the Most Holy Rosary, Holy Handmaid, Dispenser of God's Graces, Sweet Queen and Sorrowful Mother, Glorious Lady and Compassionate One, Immaculate Mother of God and Holy Virgin of Virgins." He recited a litany in which no less than thirty-eight such titles were conferred upon her: "Harbor of the Wrecked, Allayer of Tempests, Resource of Mourners, Terror of the Treacherous, Treasure of the Faithful, Eye of the Prophets, Staff of Apostles, Crown of Martyrs, Light of Confessors, Pearl of Virgins, Consolation of Widows, Joy of all Saints;" and so on.

He prayed to all the many sanctified ones who had had demons cast out, or had been tormented by them, and therefore were in position to understand the special needs of this poor woman. He said many Paternosters and then many Ave Marias. He made in the air enough crosses to have crucified all the devils in hell. All this took hours; but he never slackened, knowing that it was a test of endurance between the demon and himself, and that there was no limit to the heavenly resources upon which he could draw.

Throughout the whole ordeal he had not once spoken to Marya; he was not asking help from her, for she was a frail mortal, while this was a duel between the powers of heaven and those of hell. By special dispensation he wore a pyx, that is, a little carven box containing the all-sacred host; no demon could touch it or pass it, so the exorcist stood in a safe fortress.

He went back over the ceremony of exorcism. Again the stern commands of heaven were laid upon the infernal powers. The holy water was springled upon Marya, and she shrank from it, for it seemed to burn. Her face became red, and she was dizzy — sitting there hour after hour, staring at the priest, and hearing the thunder of his Latin objurgations in her ears. "In nomine Patris, Filii, et Spiritus Sancti!" proclaimed Father O'Donnell; and Marya was thinking as fast as her mind could move: "Yehe-shmei-rabbo-m'vorach"—"May His great Name be Blessed!" She did not know whether she should resist these spells or submit to them. She recalled with terror what the Nabataen had said, that if she, Marya, were to find herself sad in this future world, it would mean that ill was coming to Jeshu. Surely she was in trouble now; and so she was led to imagine sorrows for her beloved son!

V

Two priests arrived, carrying a precious package which one of them had brought by airplane. With many prayers it was unwrapped, and taken from the glass case; a bone of St Andrew, a most holy relic. Marya knew, by the expressions of the nuns and the priests, and by their incessant crossings of themselves, that this was a supreme moment. When the relic touched her, she felt it burn like fire, and a cry escaped her. This gave encouragement to the company of the faithful; there was a murmur of excitement, and Father O'Donnell's voice rose louder and more terrifying. "Ecce Crucem Domini, fugite partes adversae!"

Suddenly Father O'Donnell bent over and blew a strong breath up Marya's nostrils. This is known as "insufflatio," and has a never-failing effect upon all demons. The woman screamed; and the exorcist thrust the crucifix close before her face, and shouted in a paralyzing voice: "Exi ergo, impie!"

A long shudder seized Marya; she began to moan, and her eyes fell shut. Terrifyingly came a voice — not hers, a shrill, yelling voice which seemed to be everywhere in the room; a most hellish thing, so that all fell to crossing themselves as fast as their hands could move. The nuns were saying Hail Marys, and the priests were saying Paternosters, and Father O'Donnell was uplifted with triumph and faith justified. The devils were dragged forth at last!

At first nothing but shrieking. Then, as the exorcist continued to press the battle, it became plain that the demon was trying to make himself understood, using strange, outlandish words. "Quid dices?" demanded Father O'Donnell — for it is good practice to speak directly to the demons you are casting out — it puts you upon a personal basis with them, and tends to win their respect. "What are you saying?"

The yelling voice replied in what seemed to be words: "Wa-hyat-rukbatak." The exorcist turned to the professor of Arabic: "What does he say?"

The scholar was puzzled, and had to consult the large dictionary he had brought with him. His fingers were trembling so that it took him some time; meanwhile a chorus of voices was jeering and making a deafening racket, "Jahil! Jahil!" they cried, which is to say, "ignorant" — but the professor did not translate that.

Finally he declared the meaning of "Wa-hyat-rut-batak" was "By the life of thy neck!" The demon chorus hooted, in words which the professor declared were needless to render into English, and difficult to render into the Latin of the Church.

"Ask the leader who he is," commanded Father O'Donnell.

The professor had to shout the question, because of the incessant laughter and jeering. "He says they are jin," the professor translated; but instantly came a storm of hostile cries. "They are giving me a lesson," he explained. "They say jin is one, while jan are many. They are jan."

"Arl-el-aard!" shouted a voice, and the translator then said they were "earth-folk."

"What do they want?" This question was put, and the answer given: "They want the mejnun. That is the energumen — this woman whom they have possessed."

"Tell them they cannot have her. She belongs to our Holy Church.

There was another volley of protests "Wellah-billah! Wellah-billah!" shrieked the demon chorus.

"They are saying 'By God,'" explained the professor, "They mean their God, of course, not ours. They are uttering dreadful blasphemies concerning ours. They say this woman has nothing to do with our Church. They say that our Church does not know her."

"Our Church will teach them!" declared Father O'Donnell. He held the crucifix before Marya's closed eyes, and shouted: "Exi ergo, impie, exi scelerate, exi cum omni fallacia!"

He bent down again and blew into her nostrils; there started up a gale of wind in the room, wind feeling as if it had blown over iceberg, and making a whistling noise, as if it were passing through the rigging of an old-time sailing ship. The vestments of the priests were blown this way and that, and the voluminous skirts of the nuns were lifted, so that they had hard work to protect their modesty — such is demons' idea of fun. "Wellah-billah!" they continued to shriek.

But Father O'Donnell was not to be dismayed. All such developments had been provided for in the ancient ceremonial. "He who commands this rules the sea, the winds, and the tempests. Hear, therefore, and fear!"

The wind ceased, and silence fell. A new voice spoke, deep and solemn. It said: "Marya!" And then again: "Marya!"

Marya spoke in a strange, far-off tone, wholly unlike her own. "Art thou Zar?"

"I am Zar," answered the voice, speaking in the ancient Nabataean, not so easy for the professor. Marya was answering with the formulae which the sorceress had taught her. "Male or female?"

"Male," replied the voice.

"What is he saying?" demanded Father O'Donnell of his translator, and when he realized that the latter was uncertain, he cried, in Aramic: "Marya, I forbid you to speak to him. He is a demon! It is charshah!"

Nevertheless, Marya spoke. "I obey, Zar. What wilt thou?"

"Blood of the sacrifice!" thundered the voice; and suddenly Marya reached out her hands, and seized the little pyx which the priest wore upon his bosom. The company of men and women shrieked in horror, and Marya's eyes came open.

She did not see the exorcist; she saw a huge form, with a face round and big, like a newly risen moon. He had only one eye, which shone balefully from the center of his forehead. Most terrifying of all, his lower lip hung down, a great red, slobbering thing, all the way to his waist. The woman shrieked loudly; the floor beneath her began to shake, the bed on which she was seated rocked this way and that. Of course it might have been an illusion; or it might have been one of those earthquakes which every now and then shatter window-panes and knock off cornices of buildings in the City of Our Lady the Queen of the Angels. Anyhow, Marya swooned, and tumbled forward in a heap upon the floor.

VI

WHEN she opened her eyes again, she was in near-darkness and complete silence. Lifting her head, she perceived a dim reddish light, and by it she saw the face of the Nabataean sorceress, watching her steadily.

At first Marya was dazed; it was hard for her to realize where she was. She and the other woman gazed at each other.

"Well?" said the sorceress, at last. "What did you see?"

Marya had to recall. Had she really seen anything? And what was it? "Yes," she said at last, "I saw much."

"What did you see?"

"I saw the future."

"What is it like?"

Marya thought again. "A great city. People

enough for all Galilee. Buildings that touched the clouds."

"Charshah!" said the woman.

"They have chariots that move without horses or oxen. They have learned to fly in the air."

"Big charshah!" exclaimed the woman.

"Wonderful charshah!" assented Marya.

"Zar is a wonderful demon. You did well to come to him."

Marya's face clouded. "No," she said. "I am not pleased."

"What?" cried the Nabataean, instantly on the alert. "What fault have you to find?"

"Your demon had to give way to the demons of these green people. Their demons are greater than yours."

"But — you asked to see the future, and you saw it!"

Said Marya: "I did not ask to see all the future. I asked for the future of myself and my first-born."

"Zar would have done it, if it could have been done," declared the sorceress, angrily.

But Marya, a peasant woman, was not to be frightened out of speaking her mind in a bargain. "If Zar could not do it, he could have said so. I am a poor woman, and who am I, that I should pay my only first-born ram in order to see buildings that scrape the clouds and chariots that move themselves and fly in the sky? I am not concerned with things like that. I asked to see the future of myself and my son; and nothing I saw has anything to do with us."

Readers of this strange little story may be interested to know that all its details are correct — geographically, historically, philologically, and in every other way. The pictures of life in ancient Palestine have been checked to the smallest detail, and may be verified in numerous works on that subject. I mention a standard one: A Schweitzer, *The Quest of the Historical Jesus.* For the Hebrew and Aramaic phrases I have drawn upon the scholarship of my generous friend, Lewis Browne, and also a kind friend of his, a learned rabbi. The Arabic phrases are from Doughty's *Arabia Deserta.* The Demon Zar and his mother are in *Alarms and Excursions in Arabia,* by Bertram Thomas, a British political officer. The Catholic church ceremony for the exorcism of demons is from the 16th century

Latin text, to be found in the Los Angeles Public Library. It is canonical.

The story of the exorcism of demons in Iowa has been adapted from a pamphlet bearing the elaborate title: *Begone Satan! A Soul-Stirring Account of Diabolical Possession. Woman Cursed by Her Own Father, Possessed from 14th Year Till 40th Year. Devils Appearing: Beelzebub, Lucifer, Judas, Jacob and Mina. Published by Rev Celestine Kapsner, OSB, St John's Abbey, Collegeville, Minn.*This work was published in 1935, with the *Imprimatur* of the Bishop of St Cloud and the *Nihil Obstat* of the Rt Rev John P Durham; Catholics therefore will not object to my making it known. You can buy it for fifteen cents. What you are to make of the story you may ask the psychical researchers. I am content to quote the words of Hamlet: "There are more things in heaven and earth, Horatio, than are dreamt of in your philosophy."

The football game between Notre Dame and the University of Southern California took place in December, 1933. I attended it, and found myself speculating as to what Notre Dame, Neustra Señora la Reina de los Angeles, would have made of her city and her university and her football team, if she had been able to visit them after nineteen hundred years. So the little story started in my mind. I carried it around with me for four years before I wrote it. To me it is a lovely story, and deeply reverent. I hope that it may seem so to others.

OTHER BOOKS BY FREDERICK ELLIS

(Buy Direct at 35% off – Contact frederick659@yahoo.com)

Author - Jack London

MARTIN EDEN

WAR OF THE CLASSES

JOHN BARLEYCORN

THE PEOPLE OF THE ABYSS

JACK LONDON ON THE ROAD

THE ASSASSINATION BUREAU, LTD.

THE IRON HEEL

Author – B. Traven

GENERAL FROM THE JUNGLE

THE DEATH SHIP

THE REBELLION OF THE HANGED

THE WHITE ROSE

THE BRIDGE IN THE JUNGLE

MARCH TO THE MONTERIA

THE TREASURE OF THE SIERRA MADRE

Author - Carl Frederick

est PLAYING THE GAME THE NEW WAY

Authors - Frederick Ellis & Carl Frederick

THE OAKLAND STATEMENT

Author – Mao Tsetung

QUOTATIONS FROM CHAIRMAN MAO TSETUNG

Author – Upton Sinclair

OUR LADY

THE FLIVVER KING: THE STORY OF FORD-AMERICA

ONE HUNDRED PERCENT: THE STORY OF A PATRIOT

WORLD'S END I

WORLD'S END II

THE SECRET LIFE OF JESUS

THE MONEYCHANGERS

MENTAL RADIO

THE MILLENNIUM

A PERSONAL JESUS

PROFITS OF RELIGION

THEY CALL ME CARPENTER: A TALE OF THE SECOND COMING

Author – Thomas Paine

COMMON SENSE, THE RIGHTS OF MAN & THE AGE OF REASON

THE AMERICAN CRISIS

Author – Karl Marx

DAS KAPITAL

THE COMMUNIST MANIFESTO & WAGES, PRICE AND PROFIT

WAGE-LABOUR AND CAPITAL & VALUE. PRICE AND PROFIT

Author – Eugene Debs

WALLS AND BARS

Author – Jean-Jacques Rousseau

THE SOCIAL CONTRACT

Author – John Reed

TEN DAYS THAT SHOOK THE WORLD

INSURGENT MEXICO

Author – Antonio Gramsci

THE MODERN PRINCE AND SELECTED WRITINGS

Author – V. I. Lenin

THE STATE AND REVOLUTION

FIGHT AGAINST STALINISM & IMPERIALISM: THE HIGHEST STAGE OF CAPITALISM

Author – David Ricardo

PRINCIPLES OF POLITICAL ECONOMY AND TAXATION

Author – Thomas Jefferson

BIOGRAPHY OF THOMAS JEFFERSON & THE LIFE AND MORALS OF JESUS OF NAZARETH

Author – Emma Goldman

ANARCHISM AND OTHER WRITINGS

Author – Rosa Luxemburg

REFORM OR REVOLUTION & THE MASS STRIKE

Author – John Stuart Mill

ON SOCIALISM & THE SUBJECTION OF WOMEN

Author – THE HOLY SPIRIT

THE GOOD NEWS: AS TOLD BY MATTHEW, MARK, LUKE AND JOHN

Author – John Quincy Adams

THE AMISTAD ARGUMENT & THE STATE OF THE UNION ADDRESSES

www.ingramcontent.com/pod-product-compliance
Lightning Source LLC
Chambersburg PA
CBHW020942310726
48980CB00001B/13

* 9 7 8 0 9 7 9 3 3 6 3 0 0 *